Bruised Magnolias

New South, Old Politics

A NOVEL

Leila Ryland Swain

RIVER'S EDGE
BOOKS

Published in 2023 by River's Edge Books
Charlottesville, Virginia

Printed and Distributed by Ingram Spark
Available at Retail outlets, Amazon, and Kindle e-store.

About the Author

 **I grew up** in the racially segregated small town of Marietta, Georgia. My early contacts with Black people were limited to a beloved caretaker named Cora, and going with my grandfather in Calhoun to take the washing down to "colored town." I attended Agnes Scott College and Emory University in Atlanta before they accepted minority students. In a graduate program in history at the University of North Carolina I learned more about the history of racism. I began to awake after moving to Washington, DC, where I worked for Charles Weltner, an Atlanta congressman who voted for Lyndon Johnson's civil rights bill. With the War on Poverty Program headed by Sarge Shriver, I traveled throughout the South visiting Community Action Agencies and experienced the injustice at close hand.

After earning a Master's in Social Work from Catholic University, I was privileged to know a number of Black clients in clinic work and in private practice who taught me more from a personal view. In a MFA program at West Virginia Wesleyan College, a brilliant Black woman mentored me and I studied the remarkable writings of Black Americans. As I gradually learned how white supremacy and structural racial inequality worked, I was shocked to realize how unconscious I had been and then became determined to work in any way that I could to dismantle these systems.

The writing of this book both reflects my efforts in this regard, and is a vision of how "those who believe they are white" and our Black brothers and sisters can come together.

Dedication

This book is dedicated to my mother, Mary Hall Swain, who taught me to fight for racial justice.

Through her role as an educator in a small Southern town, she fostered the integration of the public schools, a difficult task. Her character and ethics shaped me to constantly work for equality and justice and a higher good for all people.

Acknowledgements

I am grateful to the West Virginia Wesleyan MFA faculty who nurtured the small gleam in my eye for this story, and particularly to Jacinda Townsend, who guided me through the thickets of writing about Black people and for enlarging my understanding of how my white skin and privilege might affect that enterprise. I'm also grateful to the Shepherdstown West Virginia Writer's Group for their helpful readings and comments. My daughter, Sarah Silverstone, is a superb critic and I have leaned on her skills. I'm grateful for Judy Waits-Allen's decisive editing work and for her support.

I have been inspired by the life and work of a Southern woman, **Lillian Smith** (1897-1966), a writer and social critic of the practices of racism in the South. A friend of Martin Luther King, Jr., she wrote *Strange Fruit*, (1944) the best-selling novel. Her book *Killers of the Dream*, (1949) concerned personal memories of growing up in the segregated South and how both Black and white children were affected.

Atlanta, Georgia, 2018

CHAPTER ONE

Friday, May 4

Blair posed in front of the full length mirror holding a teal green, tea-length *peau de soie* dress up to her skinny ribs. Melanie lounged in an overstuffed chair nearby, and Blair looked at her in dismay.

"I'm really supposed to wear this outfit?" She held it out and away from her body, evaluating it with a jaundiced eye. "Strapless" as a description of the dress was a misnomer because thin cords with no real function held up the bodice. Whalebone inserts molding to her waist and breasts would cantilever their abundance. These stays would pinch. The designer had fastened an enormous organza flower in an exotic shade of fuchsia at the waist. It resembled a rogue cabbage.

"Do these colors go together?" Blair threw the dress on the bed. Due downstairs in half an hour to greet guests coming to congratulate her husband on his nomination for governor of Georgia, her pretty face was tight.

Melanie plucked a package of Newports from her cargo pants pocket. "It's like one of those costumes from *Gone With the Wind*, Blair, and I can't believe you'd really put it on. Who picked this out for you?"

"The party planner Dick hired."

Melanie had just come back to town from Montgomery, Alabama, where she had covered the opening of the lynching museum for *Atlanta* magazine. She had volunteered for the trip, which pleased the magazine editor. Her photography was getting some nice local attention.

Melanie had always sparred with Blair's husband over political issues. Despite some personal animosity toward his wife's friend, Dick Miller admired success and saw Melanie's photography as possibly useful to him. He had asked her to come to this party, take some photos of his celebration, and then he could boast of his long "friendship" with her. Melanie knew he thought that dubious honor was a suitable replacement for cash payment. She would have to twist his arm. He was not going to like her pictures of the Democratic candidate, a Black woman, in the Sunday *Journal-Constitution*.

"Dick doesn't like smoking in the bedroom." Blair picked up the dress again. "I've almost stopped, actually."

"Dick doesn't like this, Dick doesn't like that. Jeez, Blair, what's happening to you?"

"I know, I know, you're right. How did I get myself into this? Who woulda thought he'd wind up running for governor, and as a Republican at that." Blair grimaced at Melanie. "I can do this—we will be okay."

"Yeah, it's a match made in heaven." Melanie moved to a window seat upholstered in pink brocade matching the boudoir chair seats. She rested her elbows on the window sill and looked out over the long swath of green lawn sweeping down to West Paces Ferry Road, that prized road stretching from Highway U.S. 41 on the west to the storied village of Buckhead on the east. Enormous stone and wood houses, partially hidden down endless driveways, dotted the road. The area was one of the oldest parts of Atlanta and an affluent enclave of houses like the one Blair now lived in. As Melanie drove here, she glimpsed a few of these stately residences, some like castles with turrets and flags, some decadent sprawls of stone. Magnolia trees in full bloom had dropped petals that lay on the lawns like white ghosts.

A woman pushed the door open and entered with the confident slide of a debutante on a red carpet. The party planner wore a navy ankle-length dress and had pulled her bleached hair into a high, informal pile, tendrils dangling over her ears. "Hello, ladies." Her tone suggested complicity in a secret enterprise. "Blair, can I help you with the dress?"

Dark roots lined the part in the woman's coif, and Melanie wondered if this was now a cool look, or if her hair needed a dye touch-

                    Leila Ryland Swain

up. It didn't matter to her one way or the other. She stuck the cigarettes back in her pocket, hauled herself off the window seat, and stretched. "My exit cue. See you later, Blair."

"Are you going to change clothes, Miss Rutledge?" Her cool smile dismissed Melanie as hopeless. She took Blair's dress and held it for the girl to slip into.

Melanie laughed, a hoarse croak with a smoker's taint. "No, ma'am. I ain't changing for this party—I'm just the hired help. Any place I'm not welcome in cargo pants is too fancy for the likes of me." She delighted in discarding her proper English for what she called "the language of the people" when she was in Atlanta society.

Blair, caught in folds of rustling silk, reached out her hand to clasp Melanie's. Melanie held her hand in a fake tight grip. "I'll see you in a few days, right?"

"What'd we plan—I forget, so much going on."

"You're going slumming with me—we're gonna meet at the Egg Harbor at noon on Monday, right?" Blair emitted a garbled assent through the fabric covering her head.

Melanie left the bedroom, shutting the door behind her. Downstairs, guests were beginning to arrive, mostly men, a few of them with wives. She recognized the Senate Majority leader in the Georgia legislature with whom she had gone on a few dates a number of years ago before he was married. She didn't think he saw her, and she was glad of that because he would not be pleased to see her here. Despite believing a disaster was waiting for Blair as this campaign heated up, Melanie didn't want to add any trouble. As a progressive and activist, she might be involved in things that would not shed a favorable light on Dick and his campaign. She could create a lot of difficulties for her friend. Did she want to do that?

Nobody else she recognized, but why should she? These were not her people except for a reporter from the *Journal-Constitution* whom she knew from Emory. He had been in her photojournalism class and editor of the *Emory Wheel*. He congratulated her on the growing recognition of her photographs. She poked around for a half hour, shooting pictures here and there, trying to get the people who looked important into a shot. Dick waved her over to take his picture with the current governor, whom she recognized from the newspapers. She looked into an alcove where Dick was chatting with a bald man she'd never seen before, and he didn't see her take a picture. After another fifteen minutes, she let herself out by the kitchen door. She waved to Henry, who had on a white shirt and black bowtie and arranged champagne flutes on a silver tray. His smile followed her out to her car.

* * *

After the party wound down, Dick sent Blair upstairs to take off the dress she had decked herself out in. With all the important men in the city attending, her inappropriate outfit embarrassed him, and that frozen smile! Dick turned to the liquor cabinet and pulled out his secret stash of Noah's Mill. He stared at his face in the mirror over the bar, turning his chin this way and that. He decided he looked damn fine despite a few wrinkles, which conveyed thoughtfulness and experience. He clinked the heavy Waterford crystal whiskey glass, a wedding present from Blair's brother, on his image in the mirror. Her only sibling had made a name for himself in the family brewing business, which Blair had failed to do, just as she had failed to acquire the kind of taste a woman married to him should have. Given the kind of education and proper societal coaching she had received, this was surprising and deeply disappointing to him. He had expected a silk purse, and received something far different.

Dick carried the bottle with him and sagged into a chair beside the empty fireplace to sip his bourbon. He downed several shots until he felt lubricated enough to go upstairs and deal with his wife. My God, what a fool she made of him tonight! Who was this party planner who'd put her in that dress? He thought he'd hired the best in the city, but she knew nothing about clothes and he'd ruin her reputation. He should have picked the dress out himself. It barely hung onto her gigantic boobs, the ones he once thought were erotic, and she walked like a stick going around the room shaking hands with the guests. Why couldn't she be the kind of mellow hostess, laughing and mixing

 LEILA RYLAND SWAIN

with ease, that he deserved and needed as he moved further up the ladder of politics? The governorship was only the first step.

He had clawed his way to Secretary of State, which had not been easy. He'd had to call in some chits from colleagues, secrets he'd learned about them and their corrupt shadowy doings.

Things they would never want to see the light of day. He used his knowledge coldly. He could hardly believe his good fortune to be in the running for Governor of Georgia, a nimble move. Incredible, really, that he, the son of a poor farmer from the small town of Waycross, could now be positioned to run the state.

He'd worked his way through college and law school at Emory and made important contacts at school and at the law firm where he'd reached partner in two years. The Democrats were saying he was too young and untested, but they didn't know the full story of how he got here. Nobody knew the dirty secrets he kept out of view, but he had the ability to know about the secret life of those he needed to help him get ahead. He believed he was smarter than everyone. That's what it took in a cut-throat competitive world, and he intended to win.

Secrets of a more sinister nature haunted him, but not often. The rumor he'd started about a Black law student who was too smart for his own good. The places he liked to pub crawl in Underground Atlanta and the weed and money he'd taken off the drunks. Their fault for not looking out for the lift, the dummies. And how he took down some of the Tech boys who liked to hang down there, throw cash around, feel up the Agnes Scott girls (although he felt up a few of the Scotties himself—the dumb broads often let him). Those Techies never knew who put their names in the newspaper and a smudge on their ambitions. Dick groaned when he remembered all this, and a small flutter of worry began again about what critics said about his lack of a moral compass. Did he have a moral compass? Was that necessary in politics? He warded off the confusion these thoughts brought, because he had put the devastating panic attacks he'd had at Emory behind him. For good, or so he thought.

Henry, the man they had just hired two weeks ago at Melanie's urging, came in to see if he needed anything and to pick up any remaining plates and glasses. He hoisted himself out of the chair, gave his glass to Henry, muttered good night and headed up the steps to the bedroom he shared with Blair. He stumbled on the top stair and sprawled across the carpet, scraping his face on the deep weave, his mouth tasting the fine wool lint and the dust no one could vacuum out. Henry bounded up the steps, lifted Dick, and helped him walk to the bedroom door. Dick went in and Henry waited for a few moments outside to see if his services were needed any more that night.

Blair had shed the offending gown. It lay crumpled on the floor outside the closet stretching across the width of the room at right angles to the curtained windows. She was sitting up in bed with a single sheet draped over her naked body. A damp stain blossomed on the sheet from her tears.

"Why the tears, Blair?" Dick lay down beside her without removing his clothes. "I'm the one who should be crying."

Her tears became sobs.

Dick leaned over her and said, "Shut up."

She blew her nose and sniffled but that irritated him more.

"You embarrassed the hell out of me tonight. That dress was a disaster. And no matter how many times I tell you that my name is Richard, you cannot remember." She sobbed again. He pinched her on the fleshy part of her thigh. That was his go-to solution for tears. It always worked. She yelped, slid down and turned her face to the wall.

He fell instantly into a deep sleep. When he awoke a few hours later, he was hot and got up to take off his suit. Blair was still curled in a fetal position. He turned her and began to stroke her hair with some tenderness, and then her breasts. He moved over her with a stiff erection and found her responsive to him, which in his groggy state surprised him. By all rights, she should be furious because he had been mean to her and found her unsuitable. But he didn't parse that further just at that moment. He took his pleasure and may have given her an equal amount.

CHAPTER TWO

Saturday, May 5

Melanie had improvised a darkroom in a small closet off the kitchen in the basement apartment she rented in an old but venerable house in the same block of Auburn Avenue as the Martin Luther King, Jr. birthplace. Her mother, who lived in the north of the state near the mountains, warned her the neighborhood in Sweet Auburn was not safe. But her mother never took any risks, so Melanie chose to ignore her and pushed down any fears she had. For her, it was an adventure, like a junior year abroad might have been. Immersion in another culture, another world.

Melanie loved the look of the huge old-fashioned house—the light blue clapboard, the massive front porch wrapped around three sides, the heavy cement gray trim on the windows, the rolling lawn in front. "It has soul," she told her mother, knowing she used a terrible cliché but that her mother would like it. Balancing between two worlds was not easy. Hallie Clements, a professor who owned the house, reigned in the upstairs rooms.

Melanie pulled the door shut and total darkness enveloped her. She snapped on the safety light which glowed red over the photographic equipment on a waist-high shelf in front of her. The old but still beautiful and trusted Durst enlarger presided over pans awaiting chemicals. She pulled a hair band off her wrist, scooped up her abundant red, frizzy-from-humidity hair and fastened it in a loose ponytail. No little stray hairs to wander onto the sensitive photo paper and show up as worms to spoil her finished picture. She poured developer in one white enamel pan, stop bath solution in another, and fixer in the third one. The acrid smell in her nose was familiar and woven into her being. She didn't come into the darkroom as much any more, used her Nikon camera and digital editing on her Mac for most purposes. But for some shoots she used the old Rolleiflex her dad passed on to her when he had a stroke that left him weakened.

She'd developed the roll of film from the Rollei in a canister yesterday and hung the strips with clothespins to dry on a line over the enlarger. Now she searched the images for the one she wanted to develop, found it, and threaded the film in the holder. She pulled a sheet of coated paper from a box on the shelf and placed it on the easel. She set the timer on the enlarger for twenty seconds.

Her father had taught her these things in his tiny space at the end of the back porch in their home in Resaca, Georgia. She had gone with him, John Rutledge, on back roads and around and about out in rural Gordon County, where he'd grown up. Where he'd taken his famous photographs of the people who lived back there in a community clustered around the Oostanaula River, the railroad station, and the Resaca Baptist Church. A place he called home. Love and memory went into his vision and somehow it came out in his pictures. He'd told her that by the railroad track there once was a shack used as a waiting place for the train. There were two rooms: one labeled "White" and the other labeled "Colored." He'd made a photograph of the shack, which had been selected for a book, *Bygone Georgia*, published a few years before his death.

Melanie was her father's daughter. She loved everything about photography and had honed her seeing and understanding of light and shadow and the way the camera records it. In the meditation center on Ponce de Leon Avenue she frequented, the leader spoke of one's "happy place." Photography was hers.

When the timer rang and the enlarger shut off, she put the exposed paper in the developer tray and watched the image come up. Always a magic moment when she saw the image she'd captured emerge in black and white, strangely familiar and yet somehow more (or less) than she had expected to see. When the image cleared, she moved it to the stop bath and then to the fixer and then on to the rinse bath. She only had a moment to glance at the picture and its images when the doorbell to her apartment rang. A loud, insistent, repetitive buzzing. Whoever was pushing it had an urgent agenda. She left the paper in the bath and

   LEILA RYLAND SWAIN

went out, letting light safely into the cramped room.

She squinted through the peephole in her front door and Henry Perry's face greeted her. They'd met at Emory and become friends and he helped her find this apartment. He lived nearby. She smiled and turned the lock to let him in, startled to see the grim look on his brown face. His beautiful hazel eyes were crazed, that's the way Melanie would describe them later.

"My God, what's the matter, Henry?" She held out her hand to him.

"Oh yes, my god, Melanie, my brother's out there being arrested. The cops have him in handcuffs. You know my brother, Jordan, right? He's just a kid. They won't say what's the matter, what's the charge—they just shout at me and tell me to stay away." Henry was shaking.

He had not trusted her with his emotions before. They'd hung out now and then for the past year, and then Melanie helped him get a job with Dick and Blair, a job he needed to finance his studies at Atlanta Law College. His gentle nature and superb organizational skills made him more than qualified.

At first, he balked. "Butler—that's a toady to the white man, Melanie, I can't do that. I mean, can't you imagine how weird that is for me, how historic and predictable for a Black man?"

"Look, I understand your resistance, but it will pay you big bucks for easy day's work and fund law school, let you finish." Melanie winced as she realized the job would require him to toady to Dick Miller. But her practical side won out, as she knew the advantages the work could bring him. She would make sure Blair saw to it that he was treated well. So far, so good. How could she have known then how deep Henry's resistance was and what he was capable of doing?

Melanie grabbed her pocket Fuji camera and rushed out to the street with Henry. The police were putting Jordan in the back of a patrol car. The cop put his hand on Jordan's head and banged it against the side of the door before pushing him in to topple on the back seat. Melanie got a good shot of that.

"Officer!" She took off down the street toward him. "What's going on? What did he do?" She ran up to the car and stopped short as the cop held up his hand at her.

"Lady, get out of the way. Police business." The cop and the other officer with him got in the car and moved off, slowed by people from the houses and on the street and other pedestrians who made quite a crowd around them. She shot several more pictures before the patrol car was out of range. Murmurs of conversation rose to a higher level of noise as the people talked among themselves and tried to figure out what had happened. The folks who lived here on Auburn Avenue knew Henry and Jordan, and were stumped. Not many arrests were made in this area, most of the crime around here occurred a few blocks over near stores and shops.

Melanie and Henry spoke to a few neighbors and then walked back to the house. Hallie was standing on the top step and called to them as they came closer.

"What's going on down there? What's all the commotion about?" She motioned to them to come up to her. Hallie looked frail at first glance. She was deceptive that way. Her solidity became more and more evident as one drew closer and both Melanie and Henry knew her as strict and talkative, and had never known her to be mean. She'd taught psychology at Clark for ten years, had a knack for finding good renters, and made her house an interesting place to live.

"Jordan's been arrested, Hallie, and we don't know why." Melanie went up the steps to greet her.

"Good Lord, what has that boy done now? He's been tempting trouble, I see him out there talking big, getting folks stirred up."

Henry came up the steps to stand on the landing. He was taller than Melanie, but not by much. Hallie came up to his armpit, and she stretched herself upward like a cat to look in his face. Her blue eyes flashed as she stared into Henry's eyes, which were morose as he shifted them out to take in the street and the people gathering there.

"I was afraid he would take things too far." Henry rubbed his hands together as if to wash them, to rid them of something noxious.

Melanie stood there looking at them. "What on earth are you talking about, Henry? What's going on? Has Jordan gotten himself

　　　　　　　　　　　　　　LEILA RYLAND SWAIN

into some kind of trouble? Tell me." She touched his arm and felt it tremble.

"I should've told you about it before." He looked at Hallie. "Can we go inside to talk about this?"

Hallie ushered them into her large, square living room. A wide bay window afforded a view out on the street, and the floor was covered with an enormous oriental rug. The texture of warp and woof was worn in places, which added to the luster of its muted peach, dark turquoise, and soft brown colors. Several wing chairs with rumpled down cushions covered in taupe velour stood at various angles around an antique oak table. A tortoise cat snoozed in one of them and Hallie put it gently on the floor and sat down. She waved Melanie and Henry to the other chairs.

"Shoot, Henry." Hallie leaned back and set her feet on a small stool in front of the chair. She sat straight, a coil of energy, to listen.

Henry sat forward in his chair and dangled his hands between his knees. "I don't know the whole story. Jordan's got the fire in his belly, he's been poking his nose in places where he might oughta not be looking."

Melanie snorted. "What? What places? What is he looking for?" She sat forward in her chair, echoing his movement.

"Corruption of some kind. Jordan thinks there's shenanigans in the state government, and says there's a group of the police that's become sort of like a mafia mob. He's been canvassing the neighborhood, quietly, trying to find out more. Talking to people about voting, I think."

"That could be dangerous."

"Yeah, I reckon so. I told him he was asking for trouble, but he brushed me off like I was some kind of traitor to the cause. He's become a firebrand on this subject since the last elections. I can't control him, and my parents can't either."

Hallie sat quietly through this conversation, hands folded in her lap. Her face was serene, but a sense of determined purpose played around her eyes and lips. Now she was getting animated. "I been watching him going around. I wondered what he was doing. But what can anyone do when a man catches fire but watch him burn? I hope he can get out of this, but it sure smells like he's got himself into a mess."

Melanie stood up. "Come on, Henry, we need to go see what we can find out—see if we can find out what the charges are, if he can get a public defender, get out on bail."

"Wait up, girl, I gotta go see my folks and let them in on this. They need to be involved in whatever happens. But thanks, both of you." Henry's face was grim as he gave Melanie a half-hug and patted Hallie on her shoulder. "See you later, will fill you in." He left by the front door and the two women watched him bound down the steps toward the sidewalk.

Hallie motioned Melanie to sit. "You want to help Henry, but what do you really know about him and his family? I don't mean to be intrusive here, or rude to you, but I just need to…"

Melanie blushed, a tendency she had when her feelings rose up in her without regard to her instinctive protective instincts. "I…don't know what to say. I guess you're right. I don't know a lot." She wanted to take her camera out now to record this moment here with Hallie. The expression on Hallie's face. She could extricate herself with the camera from emotionally charged moments, moments that could undo her when her verbal skills failed. She pulled the camera out of her shirt pocket. "Is there anything you want to tell me, Hallie?" She fiddled with the settings on top of the little box. "And may I take your picture, just like that, with the light coming in on your face—it's perfect Rembrandt lighting—I don't mean to be intrusive either."

Hallie laughed with her, and sat still for a couple of shots.

Melanie put her camera back in her pocket. She wanted to make a connection with Hallie, and wanted her to like her. She didn't quite know how to do that, and she felt awkward.

"I was away for a few days over in Montgomery, Alabama, talking to the people who're building a lynching museum there and photographing the site. It's moving. They've done a great job of research.

"I'd like to see it when it's done. I've read about it." Hallie smiled.

Melanie felt emboldened to linger. "You know, there was a woman named Lillian Smith—she was a radical back in the '50s and '60s—

                                   LEILA RYLAND SWAIN

ran a camp up in the mountains where she taught the truth about all this—my paternal grandmother went there for a few summers and I've been reading her books. Like most white people, I've been asleep for so many years. There's a big history that's been covered over, out of sight, it's a terrible thing, to face, I mean—as a white person, that is." She winced as she looked at Hallie, who had a stern face.

Hallie sighed. "That woman, Lillian Smith, was a friend of Martin's, you know. She supported him and he tried to protect her. She was sick with cancer and he was taking her to Emory Hospital when he was arrested the first time."

"Golly, I didn't know that! So you knew Dr. King?"

"No." Hallie's face was pensive and she looked up to the ceiling as if she saw something there. "My grandmother knew him and Coretta well. She told me nobody would ever inspire her in the same way. His preaching was fire. I do attend Ebenezer Baptist Church—his memory lingers, of course. But we have a fine pastor."

Melanie was silent, absorbing this information, wondering how it would have been to know the man.

Hallie shifted in her chair. "And now you've come to live over here and put yourself into our frame of reference. It could be educational for you." She smiled, but not with her eyes. "And be careful with Henry, you hear me? He's a fine man and I helped raise him and his brother."

Melanie couldn't interpret the tone in her voice, so she said nothing and rose to go. She offered her hand to Hallie, and she took it. After she closed the door, Hallie stood at the window watching the girl go down to her apartment. Melanie looked back at the window and gave a wave before disappearing down the steps.

She wanted to go down to the police station and ask around, see what she could find out about Jordan, but Henry's saying he had to go check with his family restrained her. She wanted to be involved but didn't want to get out in front of him on this.

She turned back to her work and went back into the darkroom she'd left so hurriedly, snapping on the light. The picture she'd developed earlier stared back at her with some sort of message. She took it out of the bath and hung it with a clip on the line strung up on the right side of the room. Last night at the party, Dick had said he wanted her to "document his lifestyle." She'd wandered around the rooms shooting groups of people who posed for her, drinks in hand—men with arms around the women they were talking to, everyone with big, maybe fake smiles. She had stepped into an alcove to look more closely at an intriguing sculpture and found Dick there talking to a man she didn't recognize. Turned sideways away from her, Dick's face was contorted and grim and he clutched the arm of the man he was with. She had taken a quick, surreptitious shot and moved away back into the main room. This photograph now mesmerized her. The man Dick was talking to looked familiar to her, but she had to search her memory for where she had seen him before.

She slipped the Fuji memory card into the slot on the side of her computer and loaded the photos she'd taken outside earlier. She had a clear shot of the policeman banging Jordan's head on the patrol car as he pushed him into the back seat, and she cropped the image and exported it into an album labeled "street shots." Then she reviewed the images she had previously loaded from her visit to the site of the lynching museum in Montgomery. Bingo! The very same man Dick Miller had in an arm hold at the party last night was in one of the pictures. He was looking at one of the hanging steel columns that represented a lynched Black person. She looked first at the picture and then at the image on her computer. Unmistakable—a lanky, middle-aged fellow with a bald head. In the museum picture, he turned sideways and the profile matched the one with Dick in the alcove. She didn't know who the man was, or what he was doing in Montgomery, or why Dick Miller was berating him. She sensed the importance of finding out who he was, but how could she do that? Blair! She would probably know.

　　　　　　　　　　　　LEILA RYLAND SWAIN

CHAPTER THREE

Henry Perry cut through several open backyards to get to his house on Howell Street, four blocks from Auburn Avenue where he had seen Jordan put in a patrol car. A pickup basketball game was underway at the corner park and the guys called to him. "Later, I'll come over later," Henry shouted. He was the best shot in the neighborhood, always sought for whatever teams composed themselves around the net. He wanted to go over and play, he wanted to bury himself in the rough and tumble game underway, forget what had happened, forget what he was afraid of. He went down Howell Street to the house where he grew up, where he was still living, even though he was full grown and a student at Georgia State College of Law. His student loan debt hung over him, and books. For Christ's sake, how much law textbooks cost—he could access some of them at the library but others had to be bought.

A Saturday. He should have been at the library. He was supposed to go back over to Miller's house, to clean up the mess from last night, he guessed. He'd go over tomorrow. So what had taken him over to Auburn Avenue? He couldn't remember now, maybe he was thinking he might see Melanie. And he did, but under circumstances other than he had imagined. Why did she want to live down here instead of uptown? He couldn't figure that out, and he couldn't figure out how he felt about her. And there was Tamila, always Tamila, who had expectations. She'd been his girlfriend for a long time, hadn't she? Did he want to marry her? He knew she wanted that. What was the matter with him?

When he rounded the corner of Howell, he could see his house in the middle of the block. A comfortable bungalow with a second story and peaked roof his grandfather had bought from a white family moving to the suburbs. Henry's mother, his only daughter and favorite child, had cared for her father there till his death a few years ago.

A tender of people and gardens and teacher of small children at the Hope-Hill Elementary School in the neighborhood—that was his mother Margaret. Henry hated to be the carrier of this bad news to her, he wished he could run away and hide somewhere until Jordan came home, if he came home. Again, as ever, Henry centered down into his place as the oldest and somehow responsible for the truant and troublesome youngest son who now was commanding the family's attention. Squeaky wheel gets the oil and be damned if that wasn't true. The troublemakers and the sick people—they were the ones who had the power. A warped power, but power nonetheless.

His mother would be in her garden, it being Saturday afternoon. Henry found her there amid the green shoots of daffodils coming up out of the earth like submarine periscopes, searching for sun, for light. He saw the reds and yellows and greens of the smock she wore in the garden and the lopsided straw hat moving as she bent to the earth before he saw her face. When she looked up and saw him coming, her face fell from its earth-working contentment to dismay, moving to the resignation of another tragedy coming her way. He winced at that look.

"It's Jordan. He's been arrested." Henry got the words out of his mouth before he failed. His mother threw her trowel on the ground and stripped yellow gloves from first one hand, and then the other.

Henry followed his mother through the back door from the garden. He couldn't tell whether she was upset or whether she had put on her false stoicism. Jordan's troubles with the police were nothing new— he'd flirted with arrest so many times. Just seemed like he wanted to be in the cops' crosshairs and then show how he could slip out—look Ma! No hands. Henry sometimes wanted to be that kid, go with him, hang out and tease the law. But he was too afraid, that's the long and short of it. Afraid of everything—he knew this about himself, hated it, felt it moving in him like a rodent scratching at the walls.

Margaret Dobbs Perry went to the telephone on the table at the end of the two-sectional sofa in the living room. She had a cell phone but only used it at school or when she was out shopping or walking. She had no intention of giving up their land line like some folks. Henry knew who she would call, knew it in his bones and knew who her

                                    LEILA RYLAND SWAIN

helper would be in this situation. Not his father, although Beko Perry was not uninterested in his family or his youngest son.

His mother dialed a number. After a few rings, she said, "Hello Walter." Henry sat down in a chair opposite her to listen.

"Jordan has been arrested."

"On Auburn Avenue, Henry saw it."

"Thank you, Walter. We'll be here the rest of the day." Henry and his mother sat looking at each other.

"Don't you need to be studying, son?" Margaret took up some crocheting from a basket beside the sofa. She began to wind a skein of blue yarn around her fingers, a deliberate and delicate movement of utter calm. Henry understood what no other observer could—Walter would take care of the situation. Walter Dobbs, his mother's older brother and Henry's uncle, whom he had grown up knowing was the one to look up to, to follow, to be up with because he would take care of things. Things like Jordan being arrested. No outside observer would understand the serenity in the living room now. Melanie had said "let's go find out," but she didn't understand how they did things here. His mother would wait to hear from Uncle Walter and then he would tell them what to do, how to address the issue. Perhaps he would even bring Jordan home. Who knew what would happen now.

* * *

A drunk sleeping it off and a man with long frizzy white hair, much older than Jordan, pacing back and forth on bare feet, already occupied the cell. Jordan noticed the man's toenails, curved ruddy daggers that clicked every time his foot hit the floor. The clicks struck a beat, like a count down to his fate. *They would charge him with something, wouldn't they? Wasn't that the way the damn justice, the so-called justice system worked?* His head throbbed where it hit the side of the police car. *Deliberate wounding, that's what it was.* He'd pushed things to this point, but he wasn't going to back down. Wait and see. Henry saw the arrest, he'd have told Mother by now. *Don't I get a phone call? Should I make a fuss about that?* His head hurt and he said, "Man, can you just sit down?" The man stopped and looked at him: "Son, we gon sit down when we get to glory but not before" He resumed his walking and his clicking, and now he began to sing some idiot song. *Damn.*

Jordan sat on the side of the shelf set up for a bed and held his head. After an interminable time in the stale air listening to the man's tuneless song, the snores of the drunk sleeping it off, and the wild beating of his heart, a cop unlocked the cell door and called his name. Jordan walked behind the cop out to the office and there was Uncle Walter. He'd never been so glad to see someone. Walter had on his stern face, his luminous eyes partly lashed, his mouth pulled in a tight line and the look sent a shiver up Jordan's spine. He might be rescued, but what other trouble was he veering into? Maybe he should stay in jail. No. He'd face whatever music Walter and his mother had in store for him.

Walter's car and driver were parked out front and the driver jumped out and opened the back door. Walter waited for Jordan to slide over the seat, and then he levered himself in with a grunt. They sat in silence as the driver navigated around through the traffic on Ted Turner Drive and then around to Courtland Street.

"You're going too far, too fast, son," Walter spoke in a low voice, his head turned away from the boy, looking out the window at the cars speeding by and the distant line of swaying trees. "They didn't book you this time, but don't think they won't get you again."

Tears swelled in Jordan's eyes, temporarily blinding him to anything but his own rage. His hands curled to fists and he pummeled his thighs like a boxer.

"You think I don't know how you feel. You think I'm old and worn out and don't have a clue." Walter turned his gaze from the window to the boy and seized one of Jordan's fists and held it clasped in his own large hands. "You may be right, but I don't think so." Walter laughed then, a deep chuckle that rose from his belly. Even as a veteran of many campaigns, he could still let his laughter fly.

Jordan thought absurdly of a Santa Claus book he'd had as a child in which the huge Santa's belly shook like a bowlful of jelly. Some of

    LEILA RYLAND SWAIN

the first words he'd learned to read. He opened his fists and spread his hands on his knees as Walter released his grip.

"I be onto something big, it's like I've hooked a big ole fish and the fish patrol won't let me reel it in." Jordan wanted to sound strong, but the words came out a little wistful and sad. He swiveled around and stared at Walter. "Ya'll think I'm just a young punk who's just causing trouble, just thinking about hisself. You think you know how I feel. But I know what Dad is doing and I'm trying to help."

Walter sighed, a deep heavy sigh with profound undernotes of anger, sadness. The sigh conveyed a sense of compromised wisdom, counseling patience for the young even as he acknowledged his own complicity and where he had failed. "Let me in on where you been, where you got to and who you talked to, so I can know why they arrested you. I will help you. I promise that." He gripped the boy's hand again and then released it.

"I think you been out of touch with us and you don't know that Mama couldn't vote in the last election. She was sure she registered but they denied it. That made her hurt and angry. I been tryin' to find out what happened—other folks been denied the vote, lots of them, all of them Black. Somebody didn't like that, didn't like me poking around. Somebody been tampering with the voter rolls, and I was about to figure out who that was."

Walter looked at him, and some kind of understanding came over his face. "I hear you, Jordan, and I'm proud of you. Let's go see your mama, and just promise me you'll back off your investigations. We'll figure it out." The car arrived at Jordan's house just at that moment.

CHAPTER FOUR

Sunday, May 6

Hair of the dog not working this morning. The beer made him tipsy all over again. Brain still fuzzy, eyes not focusing right, sobering up inevitable but seemed out of reach at the moment. Blair was sleeping in, or else she kept quiet so as not to disturb him. She knew better than to do that, and maybe she shut herself in the room where she kept her dolls. Dolls! For Christ sake, a room full of Raggedy Anns and Andys, Cabbage Patch babies with those distorted weird faces and pacifiers stuck in their mouths, American Girl dolls she got every Christmas for years. She saved every doll she ever had and brought them in trunks here when they moved in. He should have put his foot down then. Barbies! Army Barbie, Sailor Barbie, and all those country Barbies—Iceland, Mexican. A Mexican Barbie, ugh. One ancient handmade upside-down doll her grandmother made, you turn the long gingham skirt one way and there's a white doll head, turn it the other way there's a black one. What on earth was that supposed to mean, anyway?

Dick dragged himself off the sofa where he had been clicking through the morning cable news shows and tied his running shoes. His doctor said getting out and moving was the best hangover remedy he knew, sweating flushed the alcohol out. He sucked from his water bottle—not too much or he'd vomit. He gulped a couple of Advils to take the edge off his headache and went out the front door. The route he had scoped out looped around the side of the house and then to a path along a copse of mixed pines and hardwoods, mostly oak and hickory. Beaten out by other walkers and runners, the path shied along the backs of several large houses. He liked seeing what went on in the back yards, messes carefully hidden, once a woman sunbathing nude on a rickety chaise lounge. He whistled as he ran by. She sat up sharply but he sped away.

Occasionally he encountered a stout woman in a starched maid's uniform walking an Australian shepherd on a leash. He always said a polite hello but she lowered her eyes. He wondered about her as he passed by, perhaps she stalked him. Dismissed the thought as crazy. She just happened to be there at the same time on several occasions, there was no meaning to it.

Dick had measured out a mile through this section. This morning he ran to the massive hemlock marking his turn, a shaggy dark emerald presence that seemed alive, that emitted a decadent wave of forest scent to waft around his head and clog his nose. He chugged along back the way he came. He thought he would die when he began the run but now he sweated profusely and his head was clearing, so maybe the doc knew what he was talking about. When he reached his house he went around to the front to pick up the newspaper, and there was Henry, standing at the top of the steps in front of the door.

Dick couldn't figure out, first, who the hell this Black man was at his front door. His vision blurred and he thought for a moment he was back in South Georgia and being held up at gunpoint. He realized it was Henry, but why was he there—was he supposed to come today? He wiped his face with the towel tucked in his shorts and then looked up at him again. He was ringing the doorbell. What on earth was going on--why was he at the front door? Did he think he was a guest? He started toward the steps and just at that moment, the door opened and Blair beckoned Henry into the house. Dick was dumbfounded. This nigra should know his place and enter the back door. Wait until he got ahold of him. He vaulted up the steps and into the house and kicked off his running shoes, yelling "Blair, where are you?"

"In here," Blair called from the kitchen. As he entered the room, his wife handed his butler a cup of coffee.

Dick could not speak. Tentacles of anxiety and fear crept up his neck, invaded his shoulders, and a hurting began in his chest. Sweat broke out on his face and torso and he felt dizzy, so much so he sagged into a chair, choking and gasping for breath. He leaned over and puked on the floor, a pile of vomit that stank like the whiskey he had consumed. Blair leapt up and touched his back, trying to hold his head. Dick waved her away, pulled himself up, and staggered into the small bathroom off the kitchen. He shut the door and sat on the toilet seat. His heart raced and his mind veered strangely and he felt dislocated in time and space. He thought he was going to die, and almost welcomed it.

In the kitchen, Blair looked scared and bit her lip so hard it bled. "You probably need to leave for today." At the same time, she looked at Henry somehow for rescue.

"What can I do? Should I call 911?"

"No, he's had these attacks before, and I think it's panic and not his heart. But I think you need to be gone by the time he recovers himself. Let me pay you for today."

"Okay. When should I come back?"

"I'll call you. And you don't need to talk about this, do you? I mean, it's not like it's a big deal or anything, but publicity about it might not be too great right now."

"I understand."

Blair cleaned up the vomit on the kitchen floor, dry retching as she did so. The room still stank, so she lit a lavender candle and fanned smoke around. This was Sunday, and the housekeeper's day off. She sat down with a cup of coffee, waiting for Dick to either emerge or call for her. She tried to remember when the last panic attack had occurred, her memory was fuzzy and reluctant to focus on specific times past. Somehow it seemed he'd not had one for a few years, but she just couldn't recall what was going on then. In five minutes or so, Dick came out of the bathroom still shaking a bit. His face was ashen and he looked ill. He sat down opposite Blair at the table.

"Can you get me a glass of water?" He ran his hand through his hair. Blair rushed to place the water in front of him. "Whatever is the matter with you, woman? And the gall of that boy to think he was entitled to come in the front door." Dick gulped down the water and slammed the glass down on the table.

"I just wasn't thinking, Dick. We don't have to keep him on, you know."

Dick stared at her blankly. "For God's sake, he seems to be a good

                                     LEILA RYLAND SWAIN

butler, he just needs to know his place. We can take care of that." He looked around the room. "Where did he go?"

"I sent him away for today because you were so…stressed…for a while there."

"So you've created another problem—now he'll have something to hold over me. Can you get with the program, Blair? That's my question. And that car he parked out front? Where the hell did he get that one?"

* * *

Henry kept the Camaro spotless. Food wrappers, crumbs, cigarette smoke or ashes in it constituted a sacrilege. His dad had bought the car five years ago from a friend who needed cash, or so he said. Beko parked it in front of the house one day when Henry was just graduating from high school and said he could use it if he took care of it. White chassis with a black roof, a body witness to some dereliction somewhere, a usage that took the shine off but essentially left the cool, which was just the right look in the neighborhood. Henry drove it over to West Paces Ferry Road that Sunday morning because he had understood the Millers to say they wanted help with some work around the house. Heading back across town, he shook his head as the scene he witnessed washed over him again, when Mr. Miller looked like he'd had a heart attack. The image clawed at him in an ugly way. He headed out to I-75 South and merged into I-85. Traffic beastly around Georgia Tech. The job required a long commute and took serious fuel for the car. Right now the bills Mrs. Miller stuffed into his hand would cover a refill but he needed to speak to them about that expense. That is, if he went back. "I'll call you," she had said. He wondered if he wanted to detour off to the Varsity and grab a chili dog and a frosted orange, but he didn't turn off. He went there once with Melanie. It was right down her alley but he didn't feel good there with her and all the Tech boys. Yellow jackets, huh. Why the hell had he let Melanie talk him into the job with the Millers? The terror that he would bust his butt forever and never be anything but a servant rose up in his throat. He opened the window and spit out onto the highway, silently taking a vow he would not concede to this fate.

He took the usual exit off 85 onto John Wesley Dobbs Avenue and then onto Auburn. Turned up Howell and pulled up behind a car he recognized in front of his house. Walter Dobbs was here. He remembered what Walter had always told him and his brother. *"You think you all got it bad now, but this ain't nuthin'"*.

We knew even then he spoke one way to us and another one to the white men he had business dealings with and the politicians. *"Why, back in the old days,"* he would tell us, *"the dadburn so-called Jim Crow laws set down on us like a blanket of concrete and the white people controlled ever little thing about our lives. I was smart, like you are, and I got a scholarship to a college up north but I was the only person of color there. In the summers, I had to work and nobody would give me an internship like the white boys got at an insurance company or a bank, so I worked as a driver for the mayor. Now that man, he liked me but he still thought I was a nigra and all that meant. He saw me reading while he napped, and he said, "that nigra can read!" But somebody took him aside and taught him to say "nee-grow" and he was right proud of himself."*

So Walter taught them, Henry and Jordan, about what it was like, and yet how things are still the same in many ways. The police can arrest you on trumped-up charges and try to scare you out of all your efforts to keep you from becoming, to keep you in that place they assigned us so long ago.

CHAPTER FIVE

Monday, May 7

In the spring of 2015, Melanie had been maid of honor at Blair's wedding at the Cathedral of Saint Philip, a hunk of Gothic revival commanding the intersection of Peachtree Road and Andrews Drive Northwest, or "Jesus Junction," as it was popularly known. Guest list of two hundred, ten bridesmaids, ten groomsmen, little cousins in frilly dresses threw flower petals before the bride and groom, Episcopal minister on high altar in dazzling white collar gave blessings. Melanie complained about having to wear blush peach satin and high heeled pumps dyed to match and allowed Blair to pay for them, because her job as a freelance investigative reporter and photographer barely sufficed to cover her rent. The payment also compensated her for having to wear such an outfit, a one-time item.

Melanie began to suspect Blair had become entangled in a net of abuse from Dick, which she had never expected would be her plight. A month after the wedding, Blair came to her apartment in the middle of the night, driving and parking in what she considered an unsafe neighborhood (unsafe for her was outside her comfort zone). She knocked and called out. "Melanie, let me in—it's Blair. I have to talk to you. Please."

When Melanie had opened the door, a disheveled Blair with bruises on her hands and face cried and stuttered about Dick's 'moods.' "Come in, darling, come in—here, here, let me get you washed up." She hugged her stunned and hysterical friend. "What's happened?

She persuaded Blair to stay the night and made her comfortable in her double bed with a heating pad and a toddy. She stroked Blair's hair while she cried until she fell into a deep sleep.

Melanie called Dick and got the answering service, told him Blair was with her for the night, a call he didn't deserve. She fell asleep on the sofa, and when she woke, Blair was gone.

Later, Blair denied she said Dick tried to strangle her. She claimed he was drunk and accused her of having an affair with a Democratic Congressman whom she had dated during a time when she had returned the diamond ring. But that was all.

"So, you flatly deny you came over to my place that night and told me Dick was abusive? Really?" Melanie sat with Blair at the Egg Harbor Café in Buckhead on Monday after the party. She noticed heavier makeup than usual on Blair's face. She ordered the lobster scramble because it was Blair's turn to pick up the check. The wet spring had finally turned off nice and the budding peach trees lining the expansive plate glass windows shed a lambent light into the room.

"I think you've got me mixed up with someone else." Blair picked through her apple, blue cheese, and endive salad. "Yes, I've come to your apartment late at night a couple of times when I couldn't sleep and I knew you would still be up. But I just don't remember the rest of what you describe." Blair lifted her eyes to Melanie's face, and they were innocent. Melanie couldn't tell if Blair was being consciously deceptive or if she had post-traumatic stress with loss of recollection. She decided it was the latter, and sighed. "Okay." She scraped up the last bits of lobster. "Have it your way. But I hope you trust me if anything does happen."

"Nothing's going to happen. Dick will win the Governorship, and I will be First Lady of Georgia."

"And then what? What will you do—give out ceremonial ribbons and launch raft flotillas on the Chattahoochee with Diet Coke bottles? Who will you become, Blair?"

Blair looked steadily at her friend for a long time. "I don't know. I haven't really looked at the future. I think I'll be happy, helping Dick, undertaking some projects."

The waiter cleared their plates and whisked crumbs onto a blue ceramic tray with a brush. He poured Blair another glass of wine. Melanie waited for Blair to say more or to ask her about what she was up to, but Blair was silent, her face a tragic oval framed by chestnut hair gleaming with recently done highlights.

　　　　　　　　　　　　　　　LEILA RYLAND SWAIN

"Okey dokey then. I'll be off—got another assignment from Atlanta mag. This time they want me to cover the Sweet Auburn SpringFest. Right around the corner from me so I'm at home with this one. You can come down and walk around with me."

"Please be careful down there where you live. I feel frightened when I come there."

Melanie laughed. "West Paces Ferry Road McMansion row scares me more than Sweet Auburn, babe." She stood up, gathered her trench coat from the chair, swung her canvas purse on her shoulder and gave Blair an air kiss on the cheek. "I'll be seeing you—"

Something lively passed over Blair's face. "In all the old familiar places—," she crooned through a smile.

Melanie threaded her way back through the tables, turned at the exit and waved to Blair.

* * *

Blair remained at the table in the Egg Harbor restaurant after Melanie left, sipping another glass of Pinot Grigio. *Damn, they pour them short here.* Money worries popping up again. But that was in the past—Dick pulled in good money as Secretary of State, and she didn't have to think about that now. Back when she lived with her mother and father they worked hard to keep up appearances and were always fussing about pennies.

She loitered for a while, sipping her wine—she didn't want to go home yet until the cleaning people were finished. She felt guilty when she saw the two Latino women vacuuming the rugs or washing out the refrigerator, jobs she had done in the house she grew up in. Her mother would spend lavishly on outdoor Christmas decorations to compete with the tony neighbors, but make her daughter scrub the kitchen floor.

Funny, they had had a big house in Ansley Park, a good neighborhood, and she made her debut, but they had no servants. So she wasn't used to them, and Dick teased her about that, saying what a fine lady you are, you want to clean your own toilets? But he didn't mean to be cruel—he just had a unique sense of humor and she could—and would—laugh at it. She tried to think about it that way, or she would be lost.

She wondered if Dick knew her parents weren't as rich as he thought they were. They pulled out all the stops for her wedding, and her brother was making the brewery business profitable, or so he said. She wondered if that was true. She drained the wine and signed the check for the lunch, thinking how good it was to be with Melanie. Her best friend. She hoped she would come around about Dick and the governorship, for it would be awkward if she didn't.

The next morning, Dick asked her who she'd had lunch with yesterday. She said, "Melanie—it was nice."

"Why the hell does she want to live down there in the colored section of town?" Dick's tone was irritable. He snapped the *Atlanta Journal Constitution* as he folded it and laid it on the breakfast table to scan.

"I'm not sure, I think it's a money thing." She sipped the excellent Blue Mountain coffee she had just poured. She'd put on the flowered peignoir she'd been given at a lingerie shower before her marriage. It was one Dick seemed to like. "She found Henry for you, remember? And I think he's working out just fine."

"Yes, Henry is a good nigra. He works hard. But he thinks he's somebody—I hate to use that phrase "uppity nigra," but that's sort of what he is. I may have to take him down a peg or two."

"Whatever do you mean by that, Dick? I don't like the sound of that, really."

Dick looked at her hard, finished his coffee, and threw down the napkin he'd wiped his mouth with on the table. "Wife, you'd better get used to some things 'you don't like the sound of,' because I'm headed for the governor's mansion, and I'd like to think you want to go there with me."

"But, Dick, you're going to need the colored vote, aren't you, I mean, to win this election?"

"Some of it, yes. But there's not going to be a lot of coloreds voting." Blair frowned. "What do you mean?"

　　　　　　　　　　　　　　　　　　LEILA RYLAND SWAIN

"Don't you worry your pretty head about that, Blair. You worry about going down to the mall and finding yourself the most smashing dress you can. Get your nails done. That's what I need for you to do. And don't pull that pouty mouth on me. We know what we're doing, and I'm going to win. No colored vote is going to interfere with that. No Black woman can become governor of Georgia. Period."

Blair said nothing. But her head reeled and she felt a migraine headache coming on. When Dick left the house, she went back to bed with an ice pack. She had to put away the confusion in her mind or it could drag her down for days. She did the breathing Swami John taught at the yoga center: counting down from 29, starting over if she lost count, focusing on the breath and letting thoughts go. The practice calmed her and she fell asleep.

CHAPTER SIX

Saturday, May 12

The Sweet Auburn SpringFest brought thousands of people down to Auburn Avenue. They poured off the MARTA trains with children and people in wheelchairs and flooded the $5-per-day parking lots. Enterprising youths opened up side yards to visitors for three dollars and a car wash. Melanie could hardly believe how crowded the streets were and how loud the music was from the stage with mics and revved up amps. But it was May and the weather was perfect, not a cloud in the sky, the summer heat still a distant prospect. She took the Rollei on a strap around her neck and the digital Fuji camera in the pocket of her cargo shorts and strolled through the crowd, taking random shots of interesting happenings. The guy with blue paint over his dark face and a yellow and orange parrot on his shoulder, the white couple each with a black baby in a chest carrier who smiled at her and said "take our picture!"

She was to meet Blair at the MARTA Station, for she had finally coaxed her into coming down and not driving. A car would be a liability here, Melanie emphasized that and nudged Blair to do something out of her comfort zone. She could tell Blair was in a certain state of slightly hysterical indecision about coming and so she stationed herself right by the train exit to watch for her. She saw a wide-brimmed straw hat a la Scarlett O'Hara and a blue gingham sundress tripping through the exiting passengers on red wedge sandals tied around her ankles: Blair, decked out for the day's festivities. Melanie looked at her shorts and faded t-shirt that said 'Visit Dalonega Georgia' with a picture of a peach. She could have done better. Melanie greeted Blair with a brief hug and guided her out to the street and into some shade, what there was of it along the street.

"It's good to see you, Mel," Blair said. "Do I look okay?"

LEILA RYLAND SWAIN

"You look swell and will fit right in, lady friend. Let's stroll down to the music stage where I think,"—she consulted her flyer—"Devin Nash is performing, followed by Shadina and then Soul for Real."

"I feel kind of jivey—this crazy place turns me on." Blair did a few dance steps in her wedgies and held her hat against a breeze blowing down the street.

"I thought you might like it—it's not the usual Atlanta uptown scene."

They took samples from a food vendor with a sign "God is Dope," and from another selling "Tequila Hair." They giggled and went back for seconds.

"It's a different world down here." Blair twirled around, billowing her skirt.

The two continued on down the street, attracting catcalls and stares and lots of cheerful questions about whether they wanted a nice escort or not. As they drew near the stage and slid into a good listening spot, Melanie saw a face that reminded her of something, someone. She focused and couldn't remember. She clutched Blair's arm and whispered to her, "Look, who's that man?"

"Who—oh that bald fellow who's staring at me, why I know him, he's a colleague of Dick's. Look, he's turning away—guess he doesn't want to say hello." Blair pouted and turned back to the stage and Shadina, who had a funky beat going on.

"Who is he, Blair?"

"Oh, what's his name, let me think—Viktor, I think that's his name. He's some kind of political consultant, Dick talks to him all the time."

"That's the same guy that was at the lynching museum site and at your party. Let's follow him, Blair, I mean surreptitiously, so he doesn't know. He keeps turning up in strange places."

Melanie held Blair's elbow and half-guided, half-pushed her through the people swarming up toward the stage. She spotted Viktor walking rapidly down Auburn Avenue away from the crowd. A gray Bentley pulled alongside him and he jumped off the curb and folded himself into the back seat. As the car tried to navigate through the people on the street, Melanie got close enough to see his face and he looked right back at her. She had her Fuji in her right hand and she took a shot. His hand was up and he shook his finger at her. The car found an opening and sped away.

A crushing fatigue overtook the girls after an hour of relentless R&B and soul music and pressing crowds and babies crying, of wafting smells of barbeque and hot dogs, and of sun beating down on their shoulders. They slumped together on a curb while finishing melting ice cream cones—Blair had mint chocolate chip and Melanie salted caramel—and rested there until they could move again. Melanie pulled Blair up and they threaded their way through the people and down the street to Hallie's house and Melanie's cool apartment. Henry was sitting on the steps of the house.

When Blair saw Henry, she stopped and touched Melanie's arm. A sudden rush of blood to her cheeks, heart started pounding in her chest. This was all wrong, wasn't it? She thought she should surely turn and bolt back to the MARTA station, remove herself from this puzzling and confusing situation.

"It's okay, Blair. Take it easy. Nothing to get upset about." Melanie sensed her discomfort.

Blair released her hold on Melanie and took a deep breath. She could do this. Why did she think there would be some kind of trouble? A dim awareness of some understanding, some explanation she now needed grew in her mind but refused to take shape and form. She thought of her mother then, who had done her best to put her in a mold and bake her to come out like every other girl in her world. Deidre Scott from Anniston, Alabama, thought *Gone With The Wind* was the true Southern history. She read it at night to her children every night, over and over, like Pat Conroy's mother did in *Prince of Tides* and played the video of the movie often. Blair knew most of the lines by heart. *Lawsy Miss Scarlett I don't know nuthin' bout birthin' babies. Frankly, my dear, I don't give a damn.* These lines ringing in her head had defined her and helped to organize her life. But challenges to this indoctrination kept assaulting her every day now, and Blair felt the deep rumble of cracks in the foundation and

     LEILA RYLAND SWAIN

shuddered when she realized they would only deepen. Still she hung back and let Melanie take the lead. Melanie! Blair's mother loved her and her name—the exemplar of gentle womanhood in GWTW in contrast to the brash Scarlett—but Deidre didn't really know this Melanie or how different she was from Margaret Mitchell's character.

Henry stood up when he saw Melanie and Blair coming toward him and brushed off the seat of his pants and stuck his hands in his back pockets. Melanie ran up the steps to him and gave him a half-hug around his back, and Blair came up a step or two, still uncertain as to how to act in this new situation. Henry was not in the proper context here—everything was unfamiliar and scary.

"Come on, ya'll," Melanie said. "Let's go in my apartment—the heat is getting me down out here."

"I think I need to go home now." Blair was poised with her right foot on one step, her left foot on another step.

"For goodness sake, Blair, come on and have some iced tea—you're dehydrated from the sun. Just for a minute, and then I'll walk you to the MARTA station."

"Okay," Blair said with reluctance. "Just for a minute."

They all trooped down the steps to the basement and Melanie ushered them into her apartment. The darkness of the rooms enveloped them as they moved into her space and the relief from the glare rested them immediately. Melanie hurried to her small Pullman kitchen and pulled out a flowered pitcher of tea with lemons and mint floating in its depths. She found three pink depression glasses in a cabinet and brought them to her guests.

Blair and Henry still stood in the middle of the living room, visibly soothed by the rotating ceiling fan moving air around their bodies. Melanie put the glasses on a round low table circled by several comfortable chairs and gave orders: "Let's sit down, please."

Blair perched on the edge of one chair and sipped tea from her glass. "Mmm, this is good, Melanie. Where did you get the mint?" Her breathy tone and nervous laughter alerted Melanie to the extent of her discomfort.

"Henry brought it from his house – his mother's a seasoned gardener."

"Henry's mother?" Blair put her iced tea glass down on the table. She looked at Henry and seemed to take his measure anew. She shook her head. "This is hard." She laughed again, throwing her head back so that her hair swirled around her head, a laugh verging on hysteria. "I don't know how to handle this situation. Here's Melanie, my best friend, hugging a Black man who works for us—as a servant—I mean, what am I supposed to think, anyway?" She bent over and held her head in her hands.

Melanie threw up her hands in distress. "We'll figure this out, Blair." She cast a look at Henry, imploring him to do something.

Henry stood up. "Yes, it is hard. Why don't I walk you to the MARTA station and we can talk. That's okay with you, Melanie?"

"Sure. It's all good. I'll talk to you later, Blair."

Blair looked at Melanie, her eyes pleading some inchoate message, but she went dutifully out the door Henry held open for her.

Thinning crowds of people milled through the festival area and the music from several blocks away seemed to register a lower tempo, as if it were sinking to a close. The sun sank in tandem with the music, promising abatement of heat. Henry threaded his way through the street with Blair trailing him by only a few steps. Her breath seemed to have abandoned her, leaving shallow sucks of air whistling in her throat. A chaos of conflicting feelings she could not sort through attacked her mind and she could only follow the boy—the man?— who was seemingly now in charge of her.

She aimlessly thought of stopping and disappearing in the people mingling with them on the sidewalk. Tears oozed from her eyes and dropped on her blouse, making little wet spots. *There*, she thought, *there you'll see how I'm being tortured and you'll pity me and tell me I'm a brave girl. You'll take up an offering for me and rub my feet and douse me with a sweet-smelling cologne. I don't deserve this, being dragged through this misery.*

Henry turned around and called to her. "Mrs. Miller, this is just as difficult for me as it is for you."

          LEILA RYLAND SWAIN

She caught up to him and now tears were coursing down her cheeks and snot forming in her nose. "No, it isn't. You don't know my husband."

"Look, I came to work at your house to earn some money for law school. I don't have to come back, and I'm not sure I want to."

"I want to be friends with you, Melanie says you're nice, and you went to Emory and I did too, but…"

"But what?"

"I don't know, I never really thought about it, but you're a Black man and I'm a white girl and here we are walking along the street together. It's so weird. And my husband thinks you should come in the back door." She cried some more, but then wiped her nose with her long skirt and seemed to rally her nerves together. "And I don't like you calling me Mrs. Miller, even though that's my name and if you're an employee of mine you ought to, but if you're a friend of mine you should call me Blair."

Henry laughed. "You white people are so weird. How about I just don't call you either name, and when I come to your house—if I am to come back—I'll come in the back door but not for the reason your husband wants me to. I'll come in because I choose it. Okay?"

By the time they reached the MARTA station, Blair's tears were gone and a new light shone in her eyes. She felt better than she'd felt in a long time, and she waved goodbye to Henry with a light heart. Once she was on the train, she remembered she should've been home an hour ago, and Dick would be upset. And she couldn't tell him what had happened. This was the beginning of her double life.

CHAPTER SEVEN

"I don't remember when I first understood how society was unfair to black people." Melanie sprawled on a worn old-fashioned couch, propped up on several small pillows covered with flowered fabrics. Henry went behind the couch to crank open the casement windows, which let in a drift of fresh air, even though the breeze carried the warmth of late afternoon. He looked through an album of family photos Melanie had dug out of a trunk, pausing on a page here and there to ask about what he saw.

He'd seen Blair to the train and then returned to Melanie's apartment. His thoughts were jumbled. What was this thing with white people? *Maybe I'll find some answers here in Melanie's photographs. What was the saying—the pictures don't lie?* A quote from a book Henry was reading in his spare time—what there was of it—came to his mind. *"The dumbest black bastard in the cotton patch knows that the only way to please a white man is to tell him a lie."* Ralph Ellison, an author he admired, wrote this in his novel, *Invisible Man.* Henry had puzzled over this statement, said by the Black head of a Black school about his dealings with the white trustees and donors. It was an older book, and is that really the way to deal with white people?

More likely white people would lie to coloreds. That thought entered Henry's consciousness unbidden. He looked at another picture in Melanie's album to try to rid his mind of that stubborn thought, but the one he focused on was disturbing. A black and white photo, obviously old and a bit faded and overexposed, of a shack by a railroad with two rooms and over one door was a board on which was written "Whites." Over the other door, the sign said "Colored." Two different rooms for two different races, that was the way it's always been. Henry

　　　　　　　　　　　　　　　　　　　　　　LEILA RYLAND SWAIN

sighed and felt weary.

Melanie looked over his shoulder and said, "My dad took that, it's way up in the rural north of the state, out in the country where he grew up. That's the way it was then."

"It's changed in terms of some new laws, but it's not changed in terms of people's beliefs and in their hearts." Henry closed the book. "Just look at all the trouble over the voter ID laws—what is that but an effort to keep black people from voting, from having any power to affect outcomes. Effort to keep all the reins in white folks' hands."

Melanie went back to the kitchen and began to toss a salad of greens Henry had brought from his mother's garden. "I understand that, Henry. It's really so awful. My mother is fairly stuck in her white privilege, but my father's mother was "woke" for her time. She went to this camp, Laurel Falls, up in the mountains around Clayton, where a woman ahead of her time taught liberal ideas. Ideas that had not been generally accepted in those years. Lillian Smith, she wrote some books—*Strange Fruit* is one of them."

"Yeah, I read that book in lit class at Emory. I found it difficult to get through—how fixed the racial hatreds were, the prohibitions on love between a white man and a black woman."

Henry looked at Melanie, and noticed that she had changed clothes from the shorts and tee shirt she had been wearing before. Now she had on a pink shift and light streaming in from the casement windows made it transparent. He could see her unbound, round breasts, erect nipples pressing at the fabric. The sight of her firm body and careless dress aroused him despite his intention, and he squirmed in the chair to block the view. These feelings had not been a part of his relationship with Melanie before. They were pals, read the same books, and discussed politics. His mother liked her, but loved Tamila and viewed her as somewhat of a daughter.

"So what has happened with Jordan?" Melanie sat down at the table. "I haven't heard you talk about this situation."

Henry folded the length of his legs into a straight chair while Melanie dished out food on two plates. He felt relieved when the sun no longer played its tricks with her dress and so he could relax.

"Jordie is home, my uncle got him released to his custody. Apparently the police just wanted to shake him up, let him know he was treading on dangerous ground. Dangerous in the cops' eyes, anyway."

"Who is this magic uncle who could do that?" Melanie's tone was skeptical.

Henry felt irritated and defensive and couldn't contain his anger. "Yeah, that magical Negro thing--that Sambo who goes around selflessly helping white people. Except in this case, he's helping a nephew, a person of his own race."

A sheepish expression came over Melanie's face and she dropped her fork. "Oh, I didn't mean it that way, really."

"Well, but you did—that kind of thinking is so ingrained in the white mentality that it comes out, despite your conscious intentions perhaps, but it lurks there ready to pop out at the slightest opportunity." Henry sighed deeply and looked down at his plate. The food no longer interested him. Would every friendship with a white girl have to stumble across these rocky shoals?

"Henry, I'm sorry. I just wasn't thinking about that, and I will have to think about it. I mean, I want to clean up my act whenever I do stuff like that. But it does take thinking, and effort, you know."

"I know. It's like how people who have no anti-Semitic intentions at all and love Jews still can talk about jewing a price down. It's pernicious."

Melanie said nothing, but looked at Henry with both concern and fear in her eyes.

"My uncle, Walter Dobbs, was President and CEO of the Urban League of Greater Atlanta. He has built relationships across the city with every layer of government and private businesses. He has a law degree from Howard University of Law in Washington, D.C., and he is effective and has power. He was a partner in a prestigious law firm. He can work some miracles, like getting Jordie out of jail without charges, but he is not the so-called "magical Negro.""

"Okay..." Melanie's voice was subdued. "I got it. Walter's accomplishments are impressive. I'm really glad he got Jorden out

                    LEILA RYLAND SWAIN

without damaging him, going to jail is a real downer for a kid, for anybody."

The two friends finished their meal in silence. Henry excused himself shortly afterward, saying he needed to get home. Henry was almost out the door, but he turned and gave Melanie a brief hug before he was gone.

CHAPTER EIGHT

Friday, May 18

The bald man leaned his elbow on the polished mahogany bar and took the heavy glass of Scotch whiskey from the young bartender, whose bowtie was slightly askew although his white jacket was immaculate.

"I'm sorry we don't carry the Talisker 18, sir, but this Glenfiddich is excellent."

"It's fine, son, just fine." He sniffed the whiskey and took a tentative sip. "Yes, it's just what the doctor ordered. Say, do you know the Honorable Richard Miller, the Secretary of State for our fair state? Would you recognize him?"

"Yes, sir. I know him. He's a good tipper—and he likes his Scotch too." He beamed at the man he had just served as he wiped the bar with a white cloth.

"I'm to meet him here, but I'm a bit early. I will be over there reading the newspaper, if you would send him over?"

"Sure, sir."

Viktor took a seat in a massive stuffed leather chair next to a fireplace, which at this season boasted carefully arranged potted ferns shiny with an oily residue. He looked around the Cherokee Town Club, where he had not been before, and acknowledged its impressiveness. Just the right place for the Secretary of State of Georgia, and perhaps the next governor, to have a membership. He looked at his watch and noted Dick Miller was running late, maybe deliberately. To throw him off guard, show who was the dominant figure here. Viktor didn't care, he would play along with whatever agenda Miller had today. He picked up a copy of *Atlanta Magazine* on the table next to his chair and flipped through it. A photo essay by Melanie Rutledge on the process of construction of the lynching museum in Montgomery. "Damn,"

    LEILA RYLAND SWAIN

he said out loud, when he saw her picture. She was the girl with Blair at the Sweet Auburn SpringFest who took his picture through the car window. Who was she? He scanned the pictures of the site for the museum and shuddered when he saw that he was in one of those pictures—turned sideways and no full face shot, but still. What was going on?

Dick Miller walked in and headed for the bar. The barkeep pointed toward him, and Dick swiveled and looked his way. Viktor put the magazine in his briefcase and stood up to greet Miller. The two men shook hands and headed for the dining room to have lunch. Dick ordered filet mignon and Duchess potatoes, along with a bottle of 1998 Chateau Neuf du pape. Viktor ordered the vegan burger and listened intently to what Dick proposed, which seemed to him to be a joke. Unfortunately, no one had ever accused Dick Miller of joking about anything, and today's message to Viktor was dead serious.

* * *

Later in the day, Viktor met Hallie Clements at the Edgewood Corner Tavern for a drink.

He had only recently been introduced to her by a mutual friend, an Atlanta Councilman who taught at Clark College with her before running for office. The meeting was not a date, their mutual friend thought they might have politics in common and an acquaintance could be mutually beneficial to both. He may have had another, more personal, agenda. Viktor hadn't expected to find Hallie so attractive. She emanated a practical sensuousness, which was the best way he could describe her allure.

They sat in a back booth away from the happy hour crowd. Hallie told him about her work with the Voter Education Project. "I got involved through Walter Dobbs, who was head of the program through the Urban League. He's the brother of a friend of mine. Registration for Blacks was usually not a problem here in Atlanta, except in some isolated instances, but the barriers for them in rural areas are staggering. One man told us he went to register and was asked how many bubbles were in a bar of soap."

Viktor grimaced and they laughed together, agreeing that conditions were better now, but not entirely.

"A few days ago I had an interesting lunch with Dick Miller, you know, who's running for governor." Hallie nodded. "He was drinking an expensive vintage wine and insisted I have a glass too, nothing else would do, I suspect he wanted me to be infused with the tipsy spirit so that he could get drunk. And by God, that wine was spectacular, and I'm no connoisseur. But this Bud light is good enough for me."

"What good can come from drinking and talking with Dick Miller? He's a terrible Secretary of State. And a terrible person." Hallie observed Viktor over her glass of beer.

"For some reason, he wanted advice from me on managing the vote in the next election, and thinks I can help him with that. I have not disabused him of that notion—yet." Viktor scanned Hallie's face for her reaction.

An interesting mix of emotions played across her face: outrage, curiosity, wariness, some amusement. She watched him silently, waiting.

"So, I am looking for information on that aspect of the situation, and our mutual friend thought you could advise me on that."

Hallie snorted. "What do you mean, "manage the vote?" That usually means depress the colored vote. I work for registration, not repression. Or are you up to something else?"

Viktor smiled at her, hoping he'd made an impression. He liked her very much, even though that reaction also made him uncomfortable. He saw that Dick's proposal wouldn't be easy or without complicated emotions.

"I don't know much about it yet. And it just hit me that you would be a great candidate for governor yourself."

Now Hallie looked totally shocked. "Me? Whatever on earth gave you that notion?" She began to laugh, and had to cover her mouth with a napkin.

Viktor laughed with her, happy in her company. He did not consider himself handsome, although none would call him ugly, but

 LEILA RYLAND SWAIN

he had bearing, presence, and wit. The latter attribute stood him in good stead, smoothing many paths, making straight the highway, as written in Isaiah. As a compensation for early loss of hair in a male balding pattern, these qualities sufficed to make that condition not only acceptable, but a feature women seemed to love. And he wanted this woman to love him. As he sat there watching her animated face, a fear grew in his heart that she might not be interested in a white man, and if she was, depending on how things went, he might break her heart. But he pushed those feelings down.

Viktor told her he would get some information to her and have her meet a few other people "in his line of work," and asked if they could meet again here in one week. Hallie said yes. After paying the check, he suddenly remembered something and pulled the *Atlanta Magazine* he'd filched at the Cherokee Town Club out of his briefcase. He flipped to the article about the photographer and showed her picture to Hallie. "Do you know this woman?" he asked.

"Yes, that's Melanie Rutledge. She rents my basement apartment."

"Ah," Viktor said. "She's taken my picture, here." He turned the page to the lynching museum photograph and pointed to his figure. "And she took my picture again on Saturday at the Sweet Auburn SpringFest. I don't know why. She was with Blair Miller, Dick's wife, whom I met at a party at their house a couple of weeks ago."

Hallie had no answers for him, and he left her with many questions. Viktor wanted them to percolate for a while, and hoped the seeds would blossom into ripe fruit.

CHAPTER NINE

Friday, June 1

Dick put his feet up on his desk, examined his long legs, and admired the quality of the linen he'd chosen for his summer suit. Alexander at Guffey's was the best tailor in Atlanta. He would never feel ashamed of his attire when he let Alexander make those decisions. Not like that guy he had lunch with last week—Viktor whatshisname—what a slouch! Dick was sorry he'd invited him to the Cherokee Town Club when he saw his wrinkled khaki jacket and dark pants that had lint and dog hair on them, for Christ sake. And he turned out to be a vegan, too. Never trust a man who didn't like red meat, that was Dick's motto and it had always served him well.

But he was going to be useful, very useful. Dick patted himself on his back for finding and enlisting him in the cause.

He swung his feet to the floor, upsetting a pile of papers teetering on the edge of the desk. "Daisy!" he yelled to summon his secretary. Where was she when he needed her, anyway?

Daisy came running into his office and bent to pick up the papers; Dick got a glimpse of her cleavage as she did so and this mollified him for the moment.

"Daisy, where is the file on the exact match data?"

"I'll get it for you. Oh, and we have an intern for the summer. I'll have her bring you the files so you can meet her."

A young woman with fine sepia skin and short shiny dreadlocks brought the files back ten minutes later. "Hi, I'm Tamila, your summer intern." She placed the documents on his desk.

Dick was too shocked to say anything, he just stared at the girl. What on earth was happening here? Daisy handled the intern selection, and she hadn't checked this one out with him.

"Thank you. Tammie. That's what you said your name was? How

　　　　　　　　　　　LEILA RYLAND SWAIN

long have you been here?"

"It's Tamila. Just a few days, I'm getting up on the routines here."

"Ah, yes. And where do you go to school?"

"Georgia State University, majoring in poly sci."

The girl had a husky sweet voice, which Dick was perturbed to realize he found adorable.

He found himself thinking about the fairy tale in which when one girl spoke, toads came out of her mouth. When the other girl spoke, flowers floated in the air. Dick sat back in his chair wondering where on earth this fairy tale reference came from.

He put his head in his hands, confused and disturbed by the panic rising in his mind. "Get out of here, get out of here! Daisy!"

Tamila fled from his office and told Daisy that Mr. Miller seemed sick. "What did you say to him?"

"Nothing, he asked me where I was going to school."

"Okay, don't worry about it. I'll look in on him."

Dick overheard this conversation, and he was feeling better when Daisy came in his office. "So we have a colored girl for our intern." He picked up the file she had brought to him.

"Yes, Mr. Miller. She's bright and quick and an excellent student."

"Hmm. Well, I want her to work on this exact match file with me, okay?"

"Certainly, that will be fine. Do you want to talk to her now?"

"No. We'll start next week. This is a huge file—so many discrepancies in these names when compared to the identifications— they have to match exactly down to the hyphen. You know that."

"So, we have to reject any that don't match, is that right?" Daisy said with a frown on her face.

"That's the law. Now let's get to work." He plucked his linen jacket from the back of a chair, twirled it on his finger over his shoulder, and left.

* * *

Tamila Jenkins stood in the front row of the Gospel Choir of the Ebenezer Baptist Church, five feet four raised to five feet seven by green three inch heels. She lifted her book. The organ prelude had begun, and today the solo for *Take My Hand, Precious Lord* would soar through the congregation on her glorious mezzo-soprano voice. Her maroon choir robe resembled every other robe in the choir, but her voice sounded like no one else's. Maybe it was a Beyonce voice, some said. That didn't matter. She could be trusted to bring hope to every weary soul sitting in the pews, any soul that had been trampled and discouraged, oppressed and violated, during the preceding week. *Precious Lord, take my hand, lead me on, let me stand, I'm tired, I'm weak, I'm lone…* her voice rang out with the plea for divine assistance, filling every nook and cranny of the lovely old church with beauty and sorrow.

Robes rustled and books softly shut as the choir took its seats to attend to the sermon. Tamilia sank into her chair, the tune of the song still humming through her brain, pleased with her effort. The church overflowed with people and Tamila knew a room outside the sanctuary was equipped with video monitoring for the many who could not fit in the main church.

Ebenezer had become famous during the reign of Dr. Martin Luther King Jr., and now Pastor Warnock shook the rafters with his eloquence and his passion. Tamila adored him and also his wife, who was her mentor and guide.

Tamila scanned the audience, the congregation of the faithful and the curious. She recognized most of the people in the front pews and some ways back, but her vision blurred over the stretch of the room. She saw Hallie Clements sitting on the side under the stained glass window of Jesus with his shepherd's crook, holding a lamb. But who was that sitting beside her? A man she did not recognize, a stranger. She hoped she would meet him after the service.

Pastor Warnock's voice rose and fell with a cadence familiar to

     LEILA RYLAND SWAIN

Tamila. She closed her eyes and dwelt in the comforting words of salvation and the challenging words of work for justice and community. Her mind wandered as she listened, back to the last night when Henry came to her and breached her hard resolve.

From the time they could toddle out of their mothers' arms, she and Henry had played together in a gang of children in a stretch of backyards behind houses on Howell Avenue. Henry was two years ahead of her in age and then three in school because he skipped third grade. Their first date found them crammed into a booth next to each other with five other kids at Joystick Gamebar eating burgers and playing Mortal Combat and Space Invaders. For these two long time pals, being pressed against each other with bodies being jostled and rubbed awakened desire, which startled them with its energy. Their familiar faces took on a different valence, a revelation of feelings unthought of before.

Tamila recalled all this as she sorted through last night's debacle. She had not seen Henry for several weeks. He claimed his law studies but she knew from his mother that he'd also been working for Dick Miller, whom she was interning for, as a butler! And he was hanging out with Melanie down at Hallie's house too, so she heard. She'd met Melanie once or twice and although the white girl seemed friendly, a tension settled between them that had no obvious cause. Except for Henry and a struggle for his affections. Tamila would not play that game, she had been cool with Henry lately, waiting for him to declare himself.

Last night, Tamila sat on her front porch fanning herself with a paper church fan. She'd cooked all day for the church potluck the next day. Along about nine o'clock here came Henry walking down the sidewalk and climbing up the steps to her house. Her heart was beating faster and a little twist jumped around in her stomach, but she didn't stop fanning and just looked out over the lawn.

Henry slumped down in a chair next to her and groaned. Tamila fanned harder and ignored him. *Now the man wants some sympathy after his long hard day with the white girl. Wonder if she threw him out.* Her mood was not kindly toward him, and she knew he knew it.

"Baby," he said, in a tone as soft and sweet as smooth custard with brown sugar on it. "Baby, don't be mad."

"You might not want to "baby" me right now, bro." Tamila rested the fan and tapped it on her knee.

"I know, I know, I've neglected you and I'm sorry." Henry sighed, sat up in his chair, and touched her arm. She did not jerk away. "Listen to me, I need you."

This morning, in the midst of fellow choristers and the ringing words of the pastor and the yes Lords and amens responding to him, Tamila regretted that she took pity on Henry last night and let his need soften her. She grieved over her response to him, that she let him take her in his arms and pleasure her. She felt she had failed in her promise (not a promise, really, but a submission) to the spiritual guidance that faith demanded she remain chaste until marriage. Her sorrow washed over her and then faded to a muted voice, one that she could manage more gently this day.

After the service ended, Tamila stowed her choir robe in the lockers in back of the altar and headed out front to greet exiting parishioners. She saw Hallie with the man she'd spotted in the congregation and threaded her way through the throng to them. His white face gleamed palely in the midst of the sea of brown and black faces, a strong face nevertheless. Tamila hugged Hallie and put out her hand to the man, who said, "Viktor Durov here."

"Hi—I'm Tamila Jenkins and a friend of Hallie's."

"And you sing like an angel—that was beautiful."

"Thank you." Tamila restrained her curiosity about him, heightened because Hallie was holding his arm in a gesture indicating he was escorting her. She smiled brightly at both of them and said, "It's been a pleasure to meet you."

"Likewise," Viktor said. Something in the way he said this sounded in her ear like a British accent covering another foreign language that must be his native language. She picked up on these subtleties through her exquisite ear training and perfect pitch. She made nothing of it at the time but remembered this later.

CHAPTER TEN

Friday, June 24

Viktor had not counted on being photographed at the site of the lynching museum in Montgomery, but there he was in Melanie Rutledge's picture. He had driven over there from Birmingham, where he visited his mother, Olga Durov, and his sister. His father Alexei had died two years ago after teaching Russian history and language at the University of Alabama for twenty years. Viktor had flown to Omaha on business and back to Birmingham to pick up his car. He then drove to Montgomery before returning to Atlanta, where he was living. On the occasion of being spotted in Montgomery by the Rutledge girl, he was wandering the grounds where a somber confluence of monuments to the untold horrors of lynching rose.

A few years ago, a friend had shared a TED talk with Viktor, and it had banged into his consciousness like a welding iron, heating up the controversies swirling in his own brain. "We need to talk about injustice," the talk Bryan Stevenson gave in 2012, stirred Viktor because of its brilliance. A vise of conscience he was not used to experiencing trapped him, and especially given what Dick Miller was after him to do. He thought he had everything figured out and Stevenson told him he hadn't got it. A recipient of a McArthur Foundation genius award, which impressed the hell out of Viktor, Stevenson was the head of the Equal Justice Initiative, which researched and planned the lynching museum. Viktor hoped to meet him in Montgomery. This side trip showed how much the issues the talk focused on had affected him. He had no appointment to keep, he just went there, called by some inner combustion, or by a mission of duplicity, as some would later say. Viktor would always say he was a seeker of truth, and that his mission to affect the Georgia elections was an outgrowth of that search and of his sincere wish to do what was right. No one would ever understand the difficulties that had gripped him, the rope that had been cast around him to squeeze and torture him and force him to evaluate just where his loyalties lay, on threat of horrendous consequences.

The meeting did not take place, but Melanie, there at the same time, had recorded his presence. That knowledge made Viktor uncomfortable, for it might prove embarrassing, even hurtful and shameful, if it were to become public. Viktor wanted to meet Melanie, and he hoped Hallie would introduce him. He also needed to check in with Dick Miller to brief him on his trip to Omaha, where he spent two days visiting Election Systems and Software. He did not miss the irony of the two different agendas on that trip, even as he put them in separate categories.

He had presented his business card to a young man who was assigned to show him around: *George Warner, PhD, Director, Vermont Election Board, Montpelier, VT 05601.* He hated to lie, really, but he did have a small cabin in Stowe he owned with his sister that afforded a yearly ski vacation. That nugget of truth assuaged his conscience somewhat. The young man, Jack Nordstrom, took Viktor through the plant with an eagerness to show off his knowledge.

"This model here sits in the voting places in forty states. It's our best seller." Nordstrom rested his hand affectionately on a steel carcass with an implanted computer screen. "You couldn't go wrong with her."

Viktor took great interest in the wares Jack demonstrated and in Jack himself, hoping he could gain the man's confidence. Other questions Viktor had about the machines needed answers, and Jack gave them in sufficient detail for Viktor's purposes. After the tour, late afternoon had gathered around the plant and employees departed the building, walking to the parking lot headed for their cars. Jack escorted Viktor to the exit doors.

Viktor shook his hand. "Say, Jack, what's a good watering hole in Omaha? This is my first time here, and your grand tour has made me thirsty." He had not calculated this move but it seemed possible Jack was thirsty as well.

"Oh, there are several—there's one downtown that's a favorite of mine."

Viktor heard a tone in his voice—Jack was needy for company. "Want to join me? Let me buy you a brew for you for all your help."

"Sure, that's great."

Jack took him to an Irish bar named Barry O's, overflowing and noisy at happy hour, but they squeezed into a booth in the rear and ordered a couple of draft beers.

"Well, here's to a Swede and a Russian Jew meeting in an Irish bar!" Viktor raised his glass and clicked with Jack's.

"How about that, man?" Jack downed his beer in two quaffs and ordered another.

Jack was a pump ready to be primed for information and Viktor had questions in mind. "So, Jack, lots of fears out there about interfering with the machines to change votes and influence elections. You think these machines you showed me are fail safe?"

Jack sipped his beer and smiled. "Hell, no, man, if you know how to do it, it's easy."

"Sounds like you're an expert on that kind of thing," Viktor slowly sipped his beer and ordered Jack a third.

"Yep, I sure am." Jack leaned in and began to talk in a confidential tone. "See, what you want to do to hack is infect the voting management systems with a malicious code that gets spread to all the machines in that system."

"Oh, it's that simple, huh. Interesting stuff."

"Yeah, I think there are people out there who would like to do that—all they need is a little bitty UBS stick with the dirty code on it—and if they can't get the stick into a systems computer, why then they just hack into the system and add the code."

Viktor sat back and smiled. He didn't anticipate how easily an employee could be corrupted while thinking he was innocently talking to a new friend.

"So what's the answer? A paper trail?"

"That's about the only sure thing—paper backup. Ironic, ain't it—all this high-tech electronic wizardry and then you gotta have paper."

"I'm told some states refuse to do that—use paper—and I don't understand why." A feeling crept up on Viktor that he'd wrung all he could out of this knowledgeable, but rather gullible, Swede.

"That's right—Georgia's one of them—and look at the mess of their elections in 2016.

"Lots of skullduggery going on, methinks."

"Methinks so too." Viktor summoned the waitress and paid their bill. Jack said he was going to wait around for some friend who usually came in about this time, and so Viktor thanked him again, shook his hand, and left the bar in a state of satisfaction at having spent his time and money wisely. Whether he would ever use the information or not, he was happy to be informed.

CHAPTER ELEVEN

Wednesday, July 4

"**And the rockets red glare, bombs bursting in air...**" Beko Perry couldn't help singing out his approval of the fourth of July fireworks lighting up the sky over the Fourth Ward Park. "...gave proof through the night..."

"That our flag was still there..." came the chorus of voices partially cloaked in the dim light of the Perry backyard. The gathered friends and family knew their part and didn't hold back.

Beko raised his glass of sassafras beer in a toast and a hooray for the red, white, and blue.

Yes, he was still patriotic, damn it, even though the Fourth had been stolen from black people back in the days of Jim Crow. "White people couldn't stand to see freed Black people celebrating their freedom, so they squashed the festivals like they squashed so many things." He was addressing all those sitting around to watch the fireworks and daring to drink the sassafras beer, which to Beko's disgust had been declared to cause cancer. Beko knew a source for the traditional fermented root beer and he was going to die of something, so why not of sassafras beer ingestion? He scorned those who chose to give it up. "You believe the FDA, do you? Well, I believe my great-grandfather, he lived to be a hundred years old, drinking this stuff every day."

Margaret Perry put the pot luck dishes on a trestle table on the back screen porch where the food was safe from mosquitoes and flies. Ham glazed with brown sugar and vinegar cut in savory slices, potato salad from Mona next door who made it with a secret ingredient she wouldn't reveal—Margaret thought it was plain ole sour cream—several dishes of mac and cheese and many platters of turnovers and pie. They all ate well at the picnic table in the backyard and Beko personally gnawed ten chicken legs and heaped the bones by the side of his plate.

As the mosquitos began to buzz around delicate ears and ankles, Henry had brought out the citronella tubs and lit them. The smoky vapors drifted up and scented the air with familiar sweet acidic tang that hung on until the last bombs burst in the air in an outrageous final display of colored gunpowder.

"I'll have a sassafras, Beko—I don't give a damn about the FDA." The dark was now obscuring faces, but the husky voice sounding out could only belong to Walter Dobbs, who always made time for this fourth of July do.

"Thas right, buddy," Beko said as he wrestled a bottle out of the tub of crushed ice. "We got more things to worry about than that right now."

"You don't say. Well, this election coming up is shaping up to be a doozy, so I expect you're busy." Walter spoke as he wiped off the bottle of sassafras and took a swig. His wife Madie declined a sip and returned to her conversation with Margaret.

"Look," Beko said, "that racist so and so who's the Secretary of State Richard Miller is ramping up the voter suppression efforts. I got spies reporting to me, and it's bad."

"So what's the Southern Regional Council gonna do about that? Dick Miller is no easy man to wrestle with—covers hisself with grease just like a pig and slides right outa your hands. You think you have a grip, and slick Dick is gone." Walter's voice grew in volume and heat and he leaned forward in his chair to look at Beko.

"Hey, man, we working on it, you can bet your ass on that. The white man's got the levers of power, right? He's got the position and he's willing to lie and so who's the public gonna believe? Me and you? Don't make me laugh."

Margaret and Madie started listening to this exchange, which grew more excited as the conversation went on.

"Is our candidate competitive against this man?" Margaret asked. "Does she have the strength to stand up against him and expose his lies and his corruption?"

"You bet she does and will, honey. Do you have any ideas you want to share with us?" His tone was both deferential and slightly mocking.

　　　　　　　　　　　　　　　　　　　　　　　　　　　　Leila Ryland Swain

"Had to be a Black woman. That's what I know. And she has to muster the force needed to bludgeon that man. He must crumble at the sight and sound of her." Margaret, a veteran of this kind of word banter with her husband, shot right back at him with confidence

"Well let us know if you can write a speech, please."

"Should I make an appointment at your office?'

Everyone laughed and applauded Margaret. She clearly bested her mate this time. Beko joined in the applause.

CHAPTER TWELVE

Wednesday, July 18

Blair comforted herself with dolls. She arrayed the Barbies against a long stuffed cushion propped against the boudoir chair and held Raggedy Ann and Raggedy Andy in her lap. The past few weeks had been hectic and horrible. She didn't know if she loved her husband anymore. Tears oozed in her eyes but she wiped them away with Raggedy Ann's apron. She didn't want to collapse into crying, she recognized it was a weakness of hers. But weren't tears supposed to bring out the gallantry of a man? That's what she had been brought up to believe, but now maybe it was bullshit like so many things she'd been taught. She needed a clear mind and calm emotions, like her brother always had. Why were girls not supposed to be clear and defined?

That man, Viktor—what was his last name? He was up to no good, she knew it. He was so outwardly polite to her, kissing her hand like some European prince would do. Oh, she knew the type—polished to slickness and always insincere. Many men had courted her, showed interest in her, but she stuck true to Dick all those years. Why? Now anger rose in her body, she could feel it start from her sit bones and move up her spine—were these the chakras the yoga teacher talked about? She usually hated the feeling of anger and kept it hidden under a blanket of outer compliance. But now awareness was hitting in a new way, and the unfamiliar emotion assaulting her body—rage: she knew the name for it—actually felt delicious, rejuvenating.

Where would it lead her? Suddenly she was afraid and clutched Raggedy Ann to her breast for courage. The freckled doll with red yarn hair stared at her with wide button eyes and Blair pressed the doll's heart to her own, willing her rage to be guided by a right spirit.

And her mother would choose this time to come for a visit. Deidre Scott had moved back to her hometown of Birmingham, Alabama, when her husband, Blair's father, died in 2015. There she reigned from a small cottage on the rural estate of a second cousin, who tolerated her out of family loyalty. She attracted a coterie of bored would-be sophisticates drawn to her arcane style and rabid political views, which were good for entertainment, if nothing else.

At dinner, Blair told Dick that her mother seemed to have a boyfriend now. "She keeps talking about Jason when she calls—and I suspect that's an indication of her belief, anyway, that she has this male companion. She's supposed to arrive today—should already be here. And I hope she's not bringing this guy with her, if there is such a guy."

"Has she said so?" Dick asked irritably from behind the *Atlanta Journal-Constitution* he was reading at the dinner table.

"Not directly, no. But I can read her meaning from long experience." Blair picked at her chicken piccata, one of several dishes she relied on for what her mother would call a "decent meal." That's what she was supposed to provide for a husband. She really did not like to cook.

Dick had finished his meal way before Blair did. After looking at the paper, he left the table and said, "I'm going back to the office for a meeting."

"Will you be late, dear?" Blair's tone of voice did not match the endearment she expressed, and that tone surprised her as much as it surprised Dick. He looked at her with raised eyebrows.

"Don't wait up." Dick left through the back door into the garage, where Blair could hear the engine of the Porsche coming alive in a roar. She watched the diminishing taillights from the kitchen window as the car wound down the curves in the driveway to West Paces Ferry Road She was alone. A blazing July sun was sinking down behind the trees across the road, turning Blair's visible world red under its slanting rays. She loved this moment and its magic of illusion that the heavy leaves on the trees were on fire. Melanie had tried to take pictures of this phenomenon, but they never came out well. Somehow the translation onto film or SIM card turned the fiery rose color into a dead blanket of brownish-red. Blair thought it was like mana in the desert the Israelites were given when they were starving. The nourishment was only for the moment and could not be stored. *Give us this day our daily bread.*

She turned away from the window, wondering why the Bible story came up in her mind. Funny how Sunday School training came back at odd times, how something of the scripture she used to read avidly remained in her psyche. She was not disturbed by it, just curious and filled with an urgent sense of deeper waters being touched and stirred. Something she had moved away from in her life so far, something Dick ridiculed, but something she was being led back to by some invisible and forceful source. Where would it take her?

Blair heard a car in the driveway, turned back to the window, and pulled the curtain aside to see who was coming. She recognized her mother's ancient black Mercedes and a certain tilt of a head behind the wheel as familiar to her as her own hand. She shivered and tried to resist the pull of emotions she didn't want to feel. "It will be okay," she whispered, "I am strong and I am a grown woman, she cannot harm me." She said it like a mantra she repeated over and over and the cadence calmed her in the same way the dolls had. She was ready.

Deidre's car held as much baggage as she could stuff into it, but the rumored boyfriend was not part of it. "Where is this new butler when you need him, Blair?" Her querulous tone didn't bode well for the onset of her visit. Blair stifled an impulse to scream and wrestled a large suitcase from the trunk to add to the backpack she'd hoisted earlier. Thirty minutes later Deidre was installed in a bedroom on the main floor, behind the living room and down a short hall. "I only have a view out the back window, which is entirely of trees," Deidre complained as she sat on the bed to test its degree of firmness. "The bed's okay, I guess." She rose to give Blair a brief hug. "Let me unpack and freshen up a little, and I'll see you in the living room for drinks, okay?" Almost as an afterthought, she said, "It's a great big ole house now, isn't it? I'm glad to see you."

Blair realized the last time she had seen her mother was just before Deidre moved from the house in Ansley Park back to Alabama. Her brother had been there, helping with closing the house to put it on the market for sale. She had never been close to Jeffrey, who was four years older and she trembled when she heard him rant about Hillary Clinton's corruption and his love for Donald Trump. He sat her down

                    LEILA RYLAND SWAIN

and gave her a lecture about his fear of Sharia Law coming to America. His eyes flitted around the room, resting on one object after another, his anxiety stuttering his speech and his hands balled into fists, pounding his thighs from time to time to emphasize his points.

"Sharia Law is a very real threat, Blair—you're making a face, but you better watch out. Any Muslim man can have sexual relations with you if you are not wearing a Hijab, and they would cut out your clitoris."

"What's a Hijab?"

"You know what, Blair—you're hopeless. Just go back to your proms and your strange girlfriend Melanie. Yeah, she'll protect you from the Muslims."

Blair remembered all this as she put some cubes from the bar fridge in the ice bucket, set up two old-fashioned glasses, and sliced a lime. She remembered her mother liked rum with Bitter Lemon. She poured herself a glass of white wine from a chilled bottle and sat down on the sofa. July heat had been no match for the efficient AC and the house was almost too cool. Blair shivered in her sleeveless blouse.

In her reverie, Blair did not hear the motor of another car coming up the driveway and was startled when she heard footsteps on the stone front steps and the doorbell rang. She jumped up and saw a face peering in through the glass side panels on the front door. Who was this person? The face seemed familiar enough, so she opened the door. There stood Viktor whats-his-name, Dick's consultant.

"Oh, hello. My husband's not home."

"Hello, Blair, you remember me, right? I had an appointment with him tonight."

"He didn't mention that."

"Perhaps he forgot," Viktor said. "Could I talk to you instead?" His smile was bright and sincere.

Blair felt cheered, as if a friend had arrived. "So come in, then—Viktor? Is that right?"

"Yes, Viktor Durov."

Blair had not surveyed Viktor up close before. He was a head taller than she, and bald, but in a Yul Brynner kind of way, so it was not unattractive. She'd always had a kind of fascination with bald men, as well as lanky bony sort of men. Her father had been like that, he who had loved her and tried to protect her from the excesses of her mother's style.

"Would you like a drink?" She indicated the bar at the side of the living room. A well stocked bar, she knew from the way Dick had equipped it and brought in his favorite whiskeys and wines. She didn't know how to fix many drinks and didn't want to know, but was fine with a guest helping himself. Which is what Viktor Durov did. He selected a bottle of his liking and poured a middling amount in a heavy glass.

"To you, Blair—may I call you Blair? I don't mean to be discourteous."

"Oh, heavens, yes—Mrs. Miller gets to be too much for me." Blair sat back down on a plump round ottoman beside the fireplace, of course not lit in this weather.

"This is a fantastic house you have here." Viktor wandered around the room and inspected a vase here, a picture there. He picked up a bronze horse and examined it from all angles. "This steed, here, he is a magnificent specimen."

"Turn it over, it may have come from Macy's." Blair tossed her hair to lighten it around her neck.

Viktor laughed and examined her more closely. "I see you have a sense of humor, Blair."

Deidre Scott had emerged from her room, unnoticed until now, and stood beside the bar in a floor length dressing gown of some shiny floral fabric, possibly chintz. A rustling noise emerged from the garment as she moved. "Yes, my daughter—fortunately and sometimes unfortunately—has a wicked sense of humor. It's not often she shows that side to a stranger, however."

"Mother, this is Mr. Durov, Viktor Durov, a colleague of Dick's. They were to meet here tonight, but Dick must have forgotten. My mother, Deidre Scott."

"Hello, Mr. Durov." Deidre arranged herself carefully on the sofa. "Darling, would you fix me a drink?"

 LEILA RYLAND SWAIN

"I'm assuming you're referring to your daughter, Mrs. Scott, but I would be honored to prepare a drink for you. What's your preference?" Viktor put a bar towel over his arm and bowed to the ladies.

"Why thank you, I'll have rum and Bitter Lemon, please. Lots of ice—and a slice of lime."

For a few moments, the room was quiet except for the low hum of the air conditioning and the tinkle of ice in Deidre's glass.

"You know," Deidre said, putting her glass down on a side table and sitting forward on the sofa cushion, "I feel as if I've met you before, Mr.…."

"Please call me Viktor, Mrs. Scott."

"Yes, Viktor, your accent is not Southern, and yet here you are in Atlanta, doing business with my son-in-law. I am an amateur sleuth, and I suspect you are a transplant here from some other place."

"I was born in Russian Chechnya, now the Chechen Republic, but I came to this country when I was two and grew up in Birmingham, Alabama. Thus my Southern roots are strong."

"Indeed! Why, I was born in Birmingham as well. I fear it impolite to ask your age, but I suspect you are younger than I. In what part of the city did you grow up?"

"My father was a professor at the University, so we lived in faculty housing until I left home. That was my start in life."

"A professor! Oh my." Deidre became visibly agitated, her voice rose to an almost shriek. "I must talk to you about my concerns— my son tells me that we are having an invasion of Sharia Law—that horrible kind of law that comes from Muslims entering our country— and it's frightening. They will kill us women if we don't wear those awful headscarves. I hate them and refuse to wear them."

Blair focused on Viktor's face and watched as his expression turned to shock, as if he had received unexpectedly bad news, and then as it changed to what can only be characterized as a struggle not to break into uproarious laughter. Her own face turned red in embarrassment, and she jumped up and with a quick "excuse me, please" ran up the stairs to her bathroom. She sat on the toilet seat and held her head in her hands. *Why have I not ever seen so clearly how stupid my mother is!*

What an idiot! And this was the atmosphere I was raised in—I can't stand this. But I have to stand it.

Blair stood in front of the mirror and studied her face closely. She squinted and frowned and put on a silly smile. Yes, this was her face and she'd never get another one. This one would get lines and wrinkles and bags under her eyes like her mother had. *But dammit I won't put layers of cover stick under my eyes and mascara that leaks and lurid lipstick—no I will just be me.* She shook her finger at her image in the mirror and arranged her face in determination and clarity of understanding. She washed her hands, twisted her hair into a careless bun, and went back down stairs, a changed woman.

Viktor now sat on the sofa opposite Deidre and had apparently fixed her another drink. She regaled him with stories about her childhood in Birmingham and he seemed to be listening, although his posture told Blair he was bored to death. He stood when she came down the steps. His gaze seemed to lock into her soul—his eyes elevated her beyond mere girlhood to a womanhood he seemed to respect and admire. So she thought, but perhaps it was her new understanding of herself.

"I apologize—I must go now." Viktor offered his hand to Deidre, who was too sloshed to rise. "I enjoyed our chat."

Blair walked with him to the door and stepped out onto the porch with him. "Thank you for your hospitality, Blair." Viktor took her hand. "I am taken with you and your patience."

"That's what Melanie always says about me—I'm so patient." She shrugged and bit her lip.

"Melanie—your friend who takes the photographs?"

"Yes, we've known each other since college."

"I would like to meet her. She seems to like taking photographs of me."

"Yes, she does. I can arrange it."

"Good night, Blair." Viktor leaned in and gave her cheek a kiss, an avuncular kiss that surprised Blair by its lack of passion.

CHAPTER THIRTEEN

Dick thought of going to Underground Atlanta and checking out the action there, but it didn't feel quite right for the night. He drove down to the Capitol and had the passing idea he'd go to his office and work. Images of the girl, the new intern in his office, flashed through his mind. A colored girl. Who would've thought she would be hired to work with him? Everything mitigated against it, but there she was, and just as perky and smart ass as anyone. He laughed. What a joke on him, really. His old bugaboo, anxiety and panic, rumbled a bit in his gut as he considered this, but he shoved it down.

He circled around the Capitol and through the parking lot, not stopping, not wanting to go to his darkened office now, restless and wanting something else. He didn't know what that might be, so he kept driving. Soon he found himself on Martin Luther King Jr Avenue, although he didn't consciously intend to go there. He was aimless and listless, not thinking or plotting, letting the sights roll by without cognition of where he was.

Seven o'clock on a Wednesday night, summer light hanging on far into the evening and softening harsh outlines of buildings. People wandering the sidewalks looked like marionettes in this mellow light, paintings or snapshots stylized through photoshop. He knew nothing of photography, though, and wondered where that analogy came from. That was Melanie's bailiwick, and even though he disagreed with her on everything and thought her to be a malign influence on his wife, he had to give her credit for talent and accomplishment.

A red light flashed on his dashboard array. Damn! Low fuel.. How long had he been driving? An Exxon service station sign glowed on the right in the next block and he pulled the Porsche in next to the pump. He rolled down his window and sat, waiting to be served. No one came. He peered through the passenger window and although his view was truncated by the gasoline pumps, he could see figures inside the station, heads down. He waited a few minutes, and tapped his horn. Nobody came out. *Damn it, this is outrageous. Do they expect me to pump my own fuel?* Dick fumed and tapped the steering wheel. He had not pumped his own fuel for years—he only went to a service station in Buckhead where the guys knew him and jumped to compete to be the one to open the fuel tank cover. The trend to pump your own offended him. Only losers did that, and he would not submit to the humiliation such a move would lead to.

Finally, even though he was apprehensive about the kind of neighborhood he'd driven into, he got out of the car and yelled at an attendant standing just outside the door of the station. "Hey, I need some gas."

The man called back. "Just put your credit card in the slot and lift the pump."

"But I'm the Secretary of State, I don't pump my own gas."

The man laughed. "And I'm Mohammed Ali, and this is a self-serve station."

"Damnit, I'll take my business elsewhere." Dick ducked back in the car and slammed the door.

He scratched off out of the lot and back onto MLK Jr. Boulevard, trying to breathe and steady himself. He drove a couple more blocks and turned onto Auburn Avenue, rolled past the MLKJr birthplace, his breath still coming in gasps and wheezes, his head spinning. He wanted to get back to I-75 and head home, but the streets were confusing and he didn't like the neighborhood. He didn't want to admit he was lost. He turned onto Jackson Street, and the car started sputtering. He tried to accelerate but the car was slowing despite his heavy foot. He turned the wheels toward the curb and coasted into a parking place just as the car stopped. *What the hell?*

The light was dimming outside, he was far from home and out of gas. Dick rested his head on the steering wheel and cursed. He was trying to formulate a plan of action to get out of this mess when he heard the sound of music. Gospel music, sung by a choir of angels.

  LEILA RYLAND SWAIN

Am I dead? Am I dreaming? He raised his head and listened.

Sundown on a rutted, red clay road out in the country, shadows like elongated cartoon men with hats and knives, spooky screams from coyotes and owls hidden in gloomy trees. Sticky hand clasped in the big hand of Delia, swallowed in her pulsating fingers dragged along to the big light, the big sound flowing out of the church, big noise, big rays striking like lightning down my spine. Pressing against Delia's body, other hot bodies moving to the music Yes Lord, Amen, Yes Lord! Music from a divine throat a beat consuming my mind my body setting it on fire I'm taken in I'm dead and alive again and screaming with Delia til the music softens and becomes still, my heart slows its beating and we rest in the trough behind the wave of passion learning to breathe again in the pew in the small church in the new world Delia took me to and through.

Next day the beatings, thrashing of body, flaying of skin, blow after blow with a mule harness, equal passion from papa yelling, screaming about them nigger churches. Delia gone, never again, mother washing his wounds and bruises with tepid water from the outside tap, didn't I tell you not to get your father angry, son? You belong with white folks, you better than them animals out there thinking themselves all holy and what not.

Dick sobbed into his hands there in the car as he heard the gospel music from the church on the corner. He wiped his eyes and sat back in the seat. A sign was shining out from the church: Ebenezer Baptist Church. A small white cross adorned the blue background. *Ebenezer. Ebenezer.* Dick's Sunday School Bible study he hadn't thought of in twenty-five years swam back into his overwrought brain: *Ebenezer, stone of refuge. Samuel and the Philistines. Where the hell did that come from?* Dick opened the door of the car and stepped out on the street. He heard the music, the singing, coming from the church, pouring out into the darkness like a comet spreading rays through the air. He took one step, and then another, and another and found himself at the door of the church, the music pulling him into the wide clear space where he slipped into a pew at the back, still stunned and trembling from the vision, the remembrance of things past.

He shut his eyes and breathed, taking in the odor of sanctity. All churches smelled the same. He could be at the First Baptist Church of Waycross where his violent father slicked back his hair and passed the collection plate, or here—there was no difference to the nose. The song the choir nurtured rose to a crescendo and then quieted around a single voice, an angel bearing gifts, gold, frankincense, and myrrh. Dick shuddered as the voice entered him, the way Gabriel anointed Mary to bear new life. He shook his head: no. NO! An awful fate awaited him if he received the gift, and he stood and shouted: NO!

The organ stopped. The singing stopped. Someone was rushing down the aisle to him, a hand touched his arm. He looked to brush it off, and there was the colored girl from his office. She was the voice. She offered the gift, but he must refuse. She led him out of the church, down the steps to the street.

"Mr. Miller, where is your car?" The girl spoke softly to him, but held onto his elbow. "Right down there," he mumbled, "but I'm out of gas."

"Do you have Triple-A?"

He pulled out his wallet, still shaking, and delved for the card. Tamila dialed the number and spoke into her phone. The AAA truck must have been just around the corner, or there was some recognition of the name, for the rescue truck pulled up beside the Porsche not more than five minutes later. A bearded guy in a ribbed sleeveless top, hairy chest spilling out, and a train engineer's hat jumped out to fill the tank with gas. Dick stood in a daze as all this happened, eyes fixed on Tamila.

"You okay to get home, sir?" The truck driver looked him over as Dick signed his name to the papers. "Why don't you just follow me to the expressway?"

Dick assented with a nod, and climbed into his car without a word to Tamila, his eyes straight ahead on the windshield as he started the engine. He pulled out of the parking space behind the AAA truck. He watched her for a minute in the rearview mirror but when he turned the corner, she was gone.

CHAPTER FOURTEEN

Thursday, July 19

By ten in the morning, Dick Miller had done his run around the marked-out trail behind the houses, and because the weather was not too muggy for July and he was on vacation, he took his computer out to the back deck. He had designed the expansive deck overlooking the swimming pool himself and bossed the workers around as they built it, for he knew carpentry from his teen years working construction in the summers back home in South Georgia, and wanted perfection.

"Look at this, Blair, the best deck in town, worth every penny, although those workers weren't worth a damn. I had to watch them every minute or they would have cut corners—that's just the way these workers are."

"I'm surprised the guys stuck around long enough to finish the job." Blair had come out on the deck in her panda bear pajamas with a cup of coffee and the newspaper..

Dick raised his eyebrows in surprise at her unusual back talk. "Are you kidding me? They were lucky to have this job, working with the finest wood—they'd never seen this black locust lumber before and it blew their eyes out."

"It's nice alright, Dick. I like it." Blair's tone was conciliatory, she didn't want to spar this morning. Her mother was in the kitchen coddling her own egg. She'd shooed Blair away from the stove. Deidre had not slept well and her skin retained the imprint of creases in the percale sheets she'd tossed and turned in and she'd fretted about that to Blair. "Your sheets are too stiff, sort of like knives, why don't you get some silk sheets, especially for visitors?" Her hair stuck out in weird angles, having not seen a comb. When Blair had a moment of tenderness and reached out to smooth her hair, Deidre swatted her hand away. "Jiminy, just let me wake up, will you?'

"Dick, did you have an appointment with that Viktor guy here last night?" Blair looked at her husband over the top of the newspaper. The dusty lens in her glasses had him in a cloud of vapor so she'd pushed them down on her nose and looked like an owl peering out of a hole in a tree.

"No, I didn't."

"Well, he thought you did."

"What? He came round here last night?"

"Yes."

"What the hell did he want?"

"I don't know, but he was personable and we had a pleasant conversation."

Deidre pushed open the screen door from the kitchen with her elbow and managed to get through it with her coddled egg in one hand and a cup of coffee in the other, although her peignoir had slipped down her shoulder and she attempted to retrieve it with the coffee hand and tipped the cup on her arm, spilling enough dark liquid to leave a spreading spot. Blair sprang to assist her and finally secured her mother in an oversized teak chair bolstered with green canvas-covered cushions. Deidre sank into it with an exasperated sigh.

"This coffee is cold by now," she said. "I can't drink cold coffee."

"I'll get you another cup." Blair took the offending cup.

"I'll have more, too." Dick wagged his cup in an extended hand, never looking up from his computer. She took his cup, scowling at him, and returned shortly with steaming refills.

Deidre finished her eggs and warmed her hands with the cup Blair had brought. She said, "You all were talking about that Russian Viktor who was over here last night. He was really nice to me—made me a drink and we talked about Birmingham. Why, his father taught Russian at the University—would you believe we have a colony of Russians there? I am struck by that information."

Dick looked up from his computer at that and fixed his gaze on his mother-in-law. "He's no more Russian than I am."

"What do you mean? He told me he was—his parents immigrated from that place where there were all those rebels—what was it?"

    LEILA RYLAND SWAIN

"Chechnya." Blair lowered the newspaper and looked at her husband. "He came to this country when he was two."

"No way. He's putting you on. He's a phony, an imposter—he has this foreign surname and he swings it around like an ermine cape, thinking he's somebody. He's just an ordinary American, but a useful one." Dick chuckled. "And he spells his name with this "k" instead of a "c" and thinks it fools anyone. Not me. Plain old Victor Dailey from Birmingham, Alabama—at least that part about where he grew up is true."

"Dick, are you serious? He has a slight foreign accent and looks Russian to me—bald with a long nose. I don't believe you." Blair put down her paper and waved her hands around as she talked. Urgency about her speech made her stutter and spit a bit. "And what do you mean—useful?"

"He worked hard to get that little foreign tinkle in his voice and learned a few Russian words, thinks that makes him smart. We'll see if he's really smart if my plan works out."

At the sound of a motor coming up the driveway, all three of them turned to look at the car rounding the side of the house and easing to a stop. Henry's Camaro.

"I didn't know Henry was coming today." Blair hurriedly gathered up the papers and fled into the house, aware that her blue Old Navy pajamas dotted with rollicking pandas were not the garb she wanted to be seen in.

"Come on up here, Henry, and meet the mother-in-law. She showed up yesterday, and we had to take her in.' Dick waved his arm at Henry, who came slowly up the steps from the back yard.

Deidre said, "Hello, Henry." She did not take his proffered hand, indicating with a rueful smile that her hands were occupied with a half-filled cup and an empty plate. Later, she would complain to Blair that Henry did not collect her used dishes.

"So, Blair's in there making herself decent and she'll tell you what needs to be done today, okay?' Dick jerked his head sideways to underline where Henry should go, and turned back to his computer. Without a word, Henry disappeared through the back door to the kitchen.

Blair came downstairs five minutes later having put on black leggings and a loose vermillion top and twisted her long hair up into a messy topknot. She stood at the large stainless-steel double sink rinsing dishes under a flow of water from the touchless faucet, the single feature of this huge room that Henry coveted.

Blair ran her hand past the sensor in the wonderful faucet, shutting off the water, and turned to look at him. The two just stared at each other for a full thirty seconds, then Henry shifted and turned his eyes away.

"Uh, I wasn't aware you were coming over today." Blair dried her hands on a dish towel and then hung it carefully on a rack beside the sink.

"No, I know—but I came to tell you…" He stopped as the level of voices on the deck rose so that the conversation Dick and Blair's mother were having caught both Blair and Henry's attention.

Listen, Deidre, don't act stupid, you know what I'm talking about. The coloreds, god damn it, the coloreds are all against me and they must be stopped. I have a right to do any and everything I can to ensure my election, because otherwise the state will be a disaster.

Deidre's voice was quieter, timid even and they had to strain to hear her speak. *Keep your voice down, Dick, she'll hear you and you know how she is about this.*

Dick spoke more softly but still spat in crude decibels. *Look, she isn't listening—Henry's there and they're thick as thieves so stop worrying. This guy Viktor you liked so much last night is a tool—that's all he is to me. He's got the goods on the colored question, and he's going to use it or I'll know the reason why. Then he's finished—out of here—nowhere to be seen so don't get all woozy over him.*

Blair and Henry stood like frozen statues on the terracotta tile and stared at each other, eyes wide with shock. Currents of both disbelief and comprehension passed between them like actual electrical transmissions, flickering on their faces as they unwittingly kibitzed on the careless words Dick was throwing around out on his black locust deck. Deidre spoke even more softly.:

You're so clever, Dick, to think up ways you can win this election—

    LEILA RYLAND SWAIN

why, it should just be white folks voting anyway—the coloreds don't need to run things and that's what they're trying to do. But I don't believe you that Viktor is not Russian, because I know things. I looked into his eyes when he brought me my drink and I saw his soul, and dad blame it, I saw a Russian soul. I don't know how he fooled you into thinking he was just faking it. But, listen, what's Viktor going to do, really?

Dick seemed to hesitate but then he said: *He's going to adjust the voting machines—that's all I can say.*

Blair put her finger to her lips to shush Henry, who was on the verge of speaking, and they heard the click of Dick's computer as he closed the lid. *Well you just keep your mouth shut—you know you'd better—your daughter gets ideas about helping the coloreds and I just as soon not deal with her knowing about this. It will be over soon.*

A chair scraped on the deck as Dick pushed it back to get up. Blair beckoned to Henry and they fled to the living room and out to the front porch.

"Sweet Jesus, Blair, did he mean what he said out there?" Henry's face gleamed with a sheen of sweat and he kept rubbing his hands down the side of his pants in an agitated way.

"Of course he did. He's a cat with cream in his dish and nothing's going to keep him from lapping it up. What are we going to do?"

"We?" Henry spit out the words. "Who the fuck is "we?"

"Us—you and me—and Melanie—and Hallie—we have to get together and figure out how to keep this from happening, whatever it is, because I know my husband—and he's got a wicked plan." Nobody was more surprised than Blair to hear these words coming out of her mouth—"we"—and it didn't mean her and Dick. An entirely new world opened to her, and at the moment this world seemed like a black pit at her feet, into which she would likely fall.

"Blair, let's talk at Melanie's. I came over today to quit this job, and so that's it—I quit."

"Oh, Henry, what will we—I—do without you?"

"You'll find someone else to do this butler work, and we—you and me—and the others will figure out how to fight Dick and his plans."

Dick shouted from the kitchen, "Where the hell are you, Blair?"

"I'm coming, Dick, be right there." She pressed Henry's hand, and he ran down the front steps and headed around the house to his car.

When Blair got to the kitchen, Dick was cursing at the refrigerator which, when he opened it, disgorged a series of yogurt containers and plastic bags of sliced ham onto the floor.

On the deck, Deidre yelled over the sound of Henry's car, "Where is Henry going? I need him to take my plate and cup."

Blair stooped to retrieve the stuff from the floor and Dick said, "Yeah, where the hell is Henry going?"

"I don't know. He just quit." She put the ham in the refrigerator and opened a Chobani yogurt with strawberries on the bottom, grabbed a spoon to stir it with, and walked over to the door to the deck, casting a smile over her shoulder at her enraged husband.

* * *

Henry wound his way back toward his neighborhood, stopping for a burger and frosted orange at the Varsity near Georgia Tech. He usually avoided the place and the white-faced Tech boys and all their Yellow Jackets mentality, but a friend from high school studied electrical engineering there. He'd said lots of Black and Asian students were enrolled now, but certainly the dominant number of students still were white boys. Some women. So Henry thought he'd check out the Black presence at the Varsity, that palace of Caucasian jockdom, some called it jockassdom. He'd gone over there once with some Emory friends, including Melanie and two Black girls, and even though it felt like they were crashing a white party, he liked the food a lot. Liked it even while he felt some pangs of guilt that he was betraying his people by enjoying the way the burgers were seasoned and the chili and onion chunks on the dogs. Would anybody care? His mother had told him that in the past young Black boys worked as car hops there—apparently, it was thought a plum job. They'd race up to an incoming car and stick a card in the window to show it was "taken," and then

                                          LEILA RYLAND SWAIN

get the order and bring it out to serve on trays affixed to the window of the car.

Damn, why am I in this place with all this racial history? He didn't have a good answer.

Finding a stool at the bar was not hard and he slid in next to a Black student who was munching a chili dog that smelled wonderful. Henry's stomach growled, and he realized he was ravenously hungry, so he ordered a chili dog and a cheeseburger. After being assaulted by the huge red Coca-Cola signs behind the counter, he decided to go for one even though he had sworn off them after Emory. People on the campus actually were offended if you drank anything else but Coke. Pepsi was taboo. A large mirror behind the bar showed his own face shining darkly amid a lot of white skin and reflected some faces in the booths behind him. At one of the booths a man sat alone—an older man, obviously not a student. Something about the man struck Henry as unusual although he couldn't pinpoint the oddity. He was bald but that aspect seemed harmonious with the set of his shoulders, his tapered fingers holding a burger as he took a bite and then wiped his chin. Henry's food was placed in front of him and he began to eat, but his eyes kept returning to the man. Idly, he wondered who he was and if he was a professor or just someone who stopped in for a meal. The guy next to Henry saw him looking in the mirror, and his eyes followed to the man, and then he turned to Henry.

"You in his class?" the guy asked, still holding the last of his chili dog. It was dripping red goo on his yellow-gold t-shirt with the big insect on the front. He put the dog down and wiped the stain ineffectually with a napkin.

"No, I don't know him." Henry bit into his own food, careful to lean over his plate to contain the green pickle relish slathered on top. Man, so good.

"Just as well you don't. He's a professor—teaches Russian—I had him last semester and it was a tough class. He's finicky about pronunciation—like now I know how to say "vodka" right, and I don't even like the stuff. VUUD-ka, said with gusto." The guy chuckled and attacked his chili dog again. "And whoever would've thought

Khrushchev would be pronounced Cru-SHOW! on a big thrust of breath."

"What's his name?" Henry had become interested in the man because suddenly he remembered where he'd seen him before: the Georgia State law library, at a table across from him. Memorable because he was out of place there, a man older than most of the students, a shiny bald head that had reminded him of Vin Diesel. He reeked of foreign descent, although Henry would be hard pressed to say exactly what features led him to that conclusion. Bald, yes, with a large nose and searching black eyes, and wearing a black suit and carefully knotted tie that stood out among the students in assorted garb of sweat shirts and sneakers.

"Dr. Viktor Durov.

"I'll be damned, I've heard that name." *Wasn't that the guy Blair's mother and Dick Miller were talking about this morning on the deck? And I think Tamila mentioned meeting him with Hallie at church. Is this the same guy?* Henry kept eating, and soon the man paid his bill and got up to leave. He walked right past Henry's back as he left, and Henry told Blair later the man bumped him as he pushed through the aisle by his stool, and Henry was certain the act was deliberate.

   LEILA RYLAND SWAIN

CHAPTER FIFTEEN

Saturday, July 21

The dead heat of mid-July rested on all Atlanta. Henry's summer school class in Constitutional Law was dragging on for another three weeks, until his brain was over-stuffed with a heavy load of Plessy v. Ferguson and Marbury v. Madison. *All men are created equal.* Yah, that's what the founders said, except for one little unpleasant problem. It wasn't true. Skin color was what defined equality. Skin color made you a slave back then, and still defined you in this world.

Henry sat on the back steps of his house and stared out at the verdant grass he should be mowing, brow furrowed, sweat beads forming on his face and back. He was still responsible for the mowing, even though Jordan was now the age when he should begin to take it over. But Jordie stayed out late and slept late summer mornings. *Just something else to make me mad, something I have no control over. Like what the Supreme Court said—nine white men laying down the law. Took it fifty-eight years to overturn that one. But sixty-eight years after that, I'm still a butler and the Honorable Richard Miller, white man, is probably going to be governor of Georgia. What the hell am I doing?*

Henry stood up and stretched, threw the slobbered tennis ball at his feet for the mutt his father had adopted a few days ago. The back screen door slammed and Beko walked out on the porch yawning and scratching his head.

"Son, what should we name that dog?"

"Fetch and carry. Or just fetch. That's what dogs do."

Beko laughed, a guttural sound down in his throat. "You feeling down today, son? Why don't we go fishing?"

Henry lazily twisted his torso as he sank the tennis ball into the far reach of the yard, sending Fetch racing in an inane parody of enthusiasm. "Rockin' idea, dad. You got some time off?" Henry had not seen his father, really, for many weeks. He left early and came home late, exhausted and fretful, mute most of the time as he ate, and stared at the TV for an hour before sinking into bed. The fourth of July party was the last time Henry had been with a normal Beko, not preoccupied and gaunt even though he was packing on the pounds with the continual snacks he liked to consume.

"Yeah. I put the fishing gear in the truck yesterday—we gotta stop for bait. 'Cept if we're going after them monster browns I got the lures packed up."

"You know I'm after rainbows, Dad—there's always lots of them in the Hooch."

Henry ran upstairs for his hat and long-sleeved shirt—the sun would get fierce in the afternoon on the river. An invitation to fish with dad hurried his steps, such a while since Beko had wanted to, been able to, since maybe before law school began. He jumped in the truck, waving off his mother who wanted them to take sandwiches, drinks. She always fussed so but there was lots she didn't know about their fishing trip habits. Beko winked at him when she yelled, "Ya'll stay out of trouble, you hear?" Henry saw her in the rearview mirror standing in the driveway, hands on her hips, shaking her head. He waved goodbye.

First stop at the crumbling Jackson's liquor store on Rt. 20 south with stacks of all kinds of beer cartons in an entryway smelling of dead mice, almost twilight inside. Beko goes to the big cooler on the left wall and drags out a couple six-packs of Bass ale almost hidden behind the garish Budweiser displays. *So that's what we're drinking today.* Already thirsty, Henry puts the bottles in the cooler in the truck next to the fishing rods. Beko pours in a bag of ice and throws the bag of Cheetos he'd bought beside the cooler.

"I hope my old boat is still there. Been a while." Beko turned off the highway onto a rutted dirt road. The truck bounced along for what seemed like a couple of miles and turned sharply at a fence onto an even rougher road, which led finally to the river. The Chattahoochee swirled and sucked at the bank, trash strewn around, a few empty beer cans. "River's clear today—that's good." Beko headed into the scrub

     LEILA RYLAND SWAIN

along the bank, looking for the boat. The old flat-bottomed boat was still there, hiked up into a stand of paradise trees and covered with brush, the paddle dug in beside the hull. Beko and Henry pushed and pulled and got it to the water's edge—muddied to the knees—loaded the gear, and pushed off with some cursing and commands yelled back and forth.

Beko paddled close to the bank, avoiding the main current, looking for his spot. Henry waited for him to find the right place and be satisfied with it. That was the old way—wait for Beko to decide. The stirrings of something else, something new, moved in Henry's mind, something rising out of Henry's own waiting and thinking and pondering. A tiny glimmer of change, of a not-yet-understood future, rising like a bubble from his gut.

Beko hoisted the rusted motorcycle engine block by a dank rope and dropped anchor over the side of the boat. "You need me to bait your hook?" Beko had always done that for his boy, who from an early age dreaded threading the wiggling and clammy night crawlers.

"I got this, Dad." The squishy gunk that came out of the worm's belly made him sick, bile came up in his throat, but he pushed it down. The worm went on the hook without protest and Henry slung his line over the edge of the boat and watched the red cork bob in the water. Quiet held the two together as they fished, complicit in the joint endeavor, each with his own memories, dreams, angers, defeats, hopes. Henry's mind soothed and rested in the ripples of wind on the water, the sun angling higher, glinting through the trees.

Sittin' here with dad again, just like old times, but feeling strange, like an old photograph from an album, not something new and moving. World has changed and I'm still floatin' on the tide like flotsam, what the hell am I doing. Butlering, working for white folks, getting a hard-on for a white girl who talked me into doin' that?

Beko shifted in his seat, hauled his line in to check bait, broke open a Bass and tore the Cheeto bag, offered Henry some. All so familiar, it could have been a hundred times they went through this ritual, sometimes with Jordan, sometimes not. Henry went deeper into himself and felt the rumbles of the resentments he'd buried, including the disappointments he felt in this father whom he also loved. Larger than life in his childhood, a time now past. In Henry's eyes, his father shone heroic—steady, kind, and loving, and always truthful about the world outside their home as he had experienced it. But forbidden thoughts—opposite thoughts—now gnawed at him like rodents in hidden walls. *So why did Dad let Uncle Walter handle most situations for Mama? Other perceptions as years went by can't stifle them any more. Beko at the Southern Regional Council, yes, but actually in a mundane job, never advancing, content so it seemed to be a flunky, not pushing for more. Deferring to others, letting Uncle Walter be the real head of the family, be the one with the moxie, the leverage to get Jordan out of jail. Feelings hard to manage, could overwhelm me. But damn it, he's weak, and that's what I'll be if I do like him. Be really smart brain-wise, but never get ahead, waste time being a butler to a freaking racist looney politician. Makes me anxious, like Dick Miller was when he threw up on the floor. I won't barf here on the river.*

Henry took a Bass to wash down his bile, and glanced over at his father, seemingly content with just sittin' there dangling his line off the boat. He wondered if somehow Beko could read his mind, would he know his son's conflicted feelings of love and hate, would he understand? He didn't know if he could ever talk to this man who sired him about these things.

He felt invisible, not a new feeling to him at all.

When his mother first took him to Lenox Square to shop for school clothes, the world of white-skinned people did not look at them, or did so out of the corner of their eyes, wary. Henry felt invisible for the first time, and when he read *Invisible Man* years later, he remembered the shock of that sensation, of becoming invisible to himself in that crowd. In his own neighborhood, he was okay but when the white people came to the festivals and clogged the sidewalks, they acted like they owned the place and HE was the intruder. Gangs of white teens from northside high schools brought skateboards and pushed him off the sidewalk, divested him of his new jacket, and worse.

Thirteen and with a shiny new Mongoose bike, blue wheels, Beko laid it away at Dick's for Christmas morning I rode it everywhere dad said stay

     LEILA RYLAND SWAIN

in the neighborhood but I wanted to ride farther out and I felt bold and free that day when the four white guys stopped me at first they said hey boy what's a black boy doin' with a cool bike like that and they knocked me off in an alley and kicked the bike and slammed it against the brick wall left me bleeding beside my crushed Mongoose. I told dad I crashed and maybe he believed me, maybe not. I never rode that bike again even though dad straightened it out. Jordan took it for his I don't know where he rides.

Could he ever tell his father the truth, be visible to him? It seemed to him at that moment that he would not be able to, trying to sort out the relationship could actually stop his trajectory.

Sadness gripped him as he realized that he could probably do better with Uncle Walter. And the solution for what to do about the revelations he heard with Blair yesterday clicked in his mind. Yes, Uncle Walter would know what to do.

Beko jerked his line and started reeling it in, strong hands twisting, pulling, feeling the weight of the fish and testing himself against the creature still hidden under the rippling water. "Got something here, gonna try to get him in the boat, hold the net—there we go." He flipped the brown trout out of the water close to the boat and Henry swung the net under its dripping flesh. "Not a monster, but a good catch." Beko held the wet flopping fish and wrestled the hook out of its mouth, gentle but firm, not tearing the flesh, and threw the trout back out into the river. "Maybe he'll grow to be a monster, but we don't eat 'em. No telling what's in that river and in that fish. Watch your line, Henry, now, it's your turn."

Henry had laid his pole down to net his father's fish and now fumbled for the end wallowing in the bilge, reeled it in to find his bait was gone. Something was hungry out there. Beko gave him a few maggots and he threaded them on the hook and flung the line back out over the water, settling in for a wait, garnering his patience, pulling his hat lower down over his forehead against the sun. This part of the game—the sitting, the waiting, the pondering what lay below the surface—engaged him in a kind of meditative trance.

The world of books opened up about that time when my Mongoose was crushed—I could leave it all behind in absorption in other lives and other stories and other pains. Top of my class in high school—a ruckus when I gave the valedictory speech at graduation ahead of some white boy, actually he was a friend but his folks didn't like me edging him out. Scholarship to five schools, why did I stay close to home and choose Emory? I don't know. Walter told us he went off to the north to college, the only Black person in that school for a while. I didn't want that—I wanted my revenge on those bike busters through my mind and right here in Atlanta. I still want it.

A tug on the line brought Henry back to the boat where Beko was hunched beside him deep in his own thoughts. Henry saw a man he knew to be gifted but thwarted by circumstances and trying to bring some change through his work, with some success but not enough to amount to a hill of beans. Henry wanted to be more, be better, get his law credentials and slap the white power structure around a bit. He would do it, too.

Henry answered the tug on the line with a swift pull of his rod and started turning the handle on the reel, watching the bow in the line as the fish ran away with the hook in his mouth. He could see the shape just under the water as it moved, swift and sure, but doomed. Beko was alert now and when the shining broke out of the water he shouted, "thas a rainbow, son!" Henry reeled it into the boat and Beko scooped it up out of the water in the net, and they both admired the glint of colors arrayed on the fish's body and the agility with which it flopped and turned in the bilge. Henry palmed the fish and gave it an air kiss before tossing it overboard.

"The pleasure's in the catching, son, and we've done us proud this morning. Maybe time to pull anchor and go home now." Beko stood to hoist the anchor and dump it in the bottom while Henry held the paddle to steady the boat. It took an hour to get back to the landing place and pull the boat back into the brush. Sweaty, but with satisfied minds, the men got back to the house about two, surprising Margaret who had not expected them until much later.

                    LEILA RYLAND SWAIN

CHAPTER SIXTEEN

Melanie rarely visited Resaca, the town where she grew up. Nestled near the mountains in the north of Georgia, the area had undeniable beauty and she missed that. Especially in the fall when the leaves of oaks, maples, and hickories bloomed in a riot of reds and yellows and magentas. She took many photographs of this staggering beauty and had enlarged and matted a few to adorn the walls of her basement. Despite the nostalgia and the remembered beauty, Melanie's aversion to the town waxed and waned, usually in intense sequences. She had liked driving around taking pictures with her father. He'd shown her where he grew up in a house by the railroad tracks, on the Oostanaula River, where his step-mother presided over a country store and was the postmistress. His enthusiasm for cameras and lighting affected and instructed her, and his love for the scenes he documented lit her passion. He deeply felt the need to take good care of his family, but she knew he hated the work he was forced to do, for he had the soul of an artist. Five years earlier, she had gone to his funeral, and after that she stayed away. She always told friends that nothing ever happened there.

Melanie's therapist, a comfortable psychiatrist whom she called Dr. Sue, asked her about her feelings of reluctance to visit her hometown.

"I'm not sure why. My mother lives there, and I grew up there, but it felt like a prison to me. The girls in my high school mostly get married and have young children and they get together to play bridge and gossip. That's boring to me, and they seem limited." Later, Melanie thought about whether they made the better decision, to pay for their safety with their lives. And she remembered she felt rejected by these normal girls, even though she deplored their choices and outlook. Which came first? She didn't know.

Dr. Sue just nodded. Melanie thought the doc ought to have some reaction, even a mirroring statement, like: "You felt imprisoned." *Forty dollars a nod. What am I doing here? I know she's giving me a discount, but does that mean discounted responses? Shouldn't I get some kind of interpretation? Tell me what it all means?*

After one session, Melanie wandered to the Johnny Rocket on Luckie Street for a burger.

She was conflicted about eating red meat, but hungry enough, and it was cheap. *The advance from the magazine for my article on SpringFest is being eaten up—being therapied up.* She laughed at her own wit but shrugged off the worries for now. She'd always found the money she needed, and would ask her mother again. She also wanted to remind her mother about the pink pussy hat she was to knit for her. She wanted to wear it in the women's marches coming up in the fall.

Dr. Sue's office happened to be right across from the Georgia Aquarium, to which Melanie had a free ticket. The editor at *Atlanta* mag kept a jar on her desk filled with them, which she doled out like bonbons to those who curried her favor. Melanie would not have sprung for the ticket herself, even though she had wanted to visit the place. For a Saturday the place was not crowded, and the crepuscular gloom soothed her nerves. Large shapes moved through the dim watery tanks, designated cages in which they had the illusion of freedom but not the reality a vast ocean would grant.

Are they conscious of their containment? Do they move with stress-induced repetition like the polar bears do in zoos? Or as long as they're in water, they're happy? Melanie shuffled along the aisles flanking the tanks and shifted her mode of thought to the philosophical, like changing gears in a car so she could move at a higher plane, away from her distress. Dr. Sue called it "going abstract" and said it was a way Melanie protected herself. "A defensive maneuver" was another way she put it. *What's wrong with defending myself anyway?* She sidled by a tank full of sharks milling around and one of the creatures poked its fierce face right at her as if to say, "If it weren't for this wall…" *Danger everywhere.* She laughed loudly, causing an attendant to give her a severe look.

                    LEILA RYLAND SWAIN

She wandered in and out of a clever pod built so the grinning dolphins swam up to the acrylic barrier, flirting, giving the illusion you were playing with them. *Illusion. I'd like to really swim with them, play with them.* She angled the camera to cut down reflection and took a few shots of bottlenoses getting snacks. Moving on to a long tunnel under the plexiglass, she stepped onto the moving walkway and cringed to realize the overhead barrier held an enormous amount of water. *How much does water weigh? How did they make that acrylic so strong?* The brochure she'd picked up said the plexiglass was two feet thick. She measured that with her hands.

She stepped off the moving plank into an alcove where you felt you were in the water, even though you weren't. No flash allowed, but she set the camera to RAW format so she could edit the film later to dial back overexposed highlights and lighten the deep shadows. Snapping with a fast shutter speed, she turned and bent to catch what might be weird but perhaps wonderful shots of the monstrous, implausible whale sharks. She'd never heard of such a creature and couldn't stop watching how the mammoth lumbering forms were transformed into clumsy ballerinas in the water.

The water. She'd read a story called *The Disobedience of Water* for English Lit, and the truth of that title struck her now—the whale shark would flounder and flap on land, but the water freed it, the water that broke the rules of land, of gravity. When she was a child, the family took summer vacations on St. Simons Island off the coast. One of her earliest memories was of arriving at the cottage on the beach behind the dunes and heading straight for the water, seduced by the sound of the waves. She made a beeline down through the dune and the grass, getting sand spurs in her feet. Her first escape. A frantic mother. *A scary prospect to have a daughter loosening her corset.* Melanie giggled as she took a final photograph of a whale shark, which had swum up close to the barrier and shined a single, round and curious eye at her. Maybe the shark was glad to be in its tank, after all, for in the open sea he would have to travel with others, find food, and set a direction, perhaps reproduce his kind. She shivered, suddenly cold in the air conditioned air of the aquarium. Freedom had its costs.

Out on Baker Street, the afternoon heat, humidity, and traffic hit her like the acrylic wall of the aquarium breaking around her. She stumbled, stunned and senseless, down the hot pavement for a block, overcome by dread and loneliness. Dizziness assailed her and forced her to lean against the window of Johnny Rocket's and drop her head. After a moment or two, she was able to go into the place, sit at the end of the counter, and order a coke. "Are you all right, ma'am?" The waiter placed the glass in front of her. She was unable to share any portion of her misery with the boy in a white paper cap.

Fortified with cold sweet soda and burping a little, Melanie started walking back to her apartment slowly, letting the famous coke syrup cure her, as it always had done. Her mother dosed every childhood ailment with it. Buckets of ice and bottled coke dotted the Emory campus, or Coca-Cola U, as some called it because of the beneficent endowments of the company to the university. The "co-cola" largess would be found especially on moving-into-dorm days, when parents were around. Now, even though Melanie suspected the coke acted mostly as placebo—cocaine removed from the formula years ago— the effect worked in her psyche. Riding the wave of warnings about aspartame, she only drank it occasionally in a crisis, like today. Like the occasional cigarette she smoked, exquisite on the first puff but downhill from there, becoming increasingly unpleasant and guilt-inducing.

A familiar walk to her, less than two miles, the path took her through the Centennial Olympic Park, twenty acres of green trees and gushing fountains in the middle of the city. The Wednesday Winddown concerts were over for the season, but she had kibitzed on several in June and had taken some covert photographs of the musicians. She'd never bought a ticket or sat through a performance. Usually an overflow crowd of mostly white people filled the park, a few Black families with coolers. She'd attended another kind of concert here with Henry and some other students from Emory a few years ago. The popular band Outkast lit up the night with their delirious hip-hop, and she'd stood shoulder to shoulder with fired-up Black people, feeling like an intruder but being caught up in the electricity of the music. The performers Big Boi and Andre 3000 with his white wig

                                        LEILA RYLAND SWAIN

and sunglasses galvanized the masses of people crammed into the park. The newspaper called the number twenty thousand or more.

She had never felt so white as when she was with this large group of Black people. Self-consciousness crept up her spine and made her uneasy. She loved being here, had wanted to be here, but she couldn't hatch out of her shell of white cultural indoctrination. That's what she labeled it. So her feeling of isolation intensified as she struggled with the paradox of her whiteness and whether she was "privileged" by her color. Her Black sorority sister Annette from Baltimore dinged her with, "You're skating on your white privilege, girl," with a grin that conveyed criticism as well as a refreshing frankness. *She was right, even though I didn't like to hear it. Because I didn't know how to change who I was, how I operated, she called me out on something I had no control over.* Melanie didn't like to think about it, really. But the thoughts, and things said to her, had a stubborn reality she couldn't dismiss.

CHAPTER SEVENTEEN

The sun streamed through the window over Dorothy's kitchen sink where she had hung curtains, checkered red and white cotton trimmed in red rick rack. She had made the curtains on her Singer, which had belonged to her mother and was still in perfect working condition. Fancier model sewing machines had come on the market, but she didn't want to learn all the new gadgets. They don't make things like they used to, she often said. Her standing Kitchenaid mixer was twenty-five years old and kneaded dough as well as when it was new, whereas her young neighbor's new mixer broke after two years in use. She held reliability as an important virtue.

She used to make her clothes and dresses for Melanie, but didn't do that anymore. She loved shopping at the mall and finding outfits that suited her taste, like the yellow dotted swiss dress she wore today. An opaque cotton slip of the same color lined the dress to provide modesty, and her newish sandals opened at the toe, allowing one painted nail to peek out.

Dorothy sat at the kitchen table to prepare her Sunday School lesson. She'd taught an adult class at the First Baptist Church in Resaca for twenty years and she knew what the people wanted to hear and discuss. The scripture for tomorrow's class, dictated from the syllabus the minister provided, vexed her because it seemed inscrutable and difficult: A Letter to the Roman Church From the Apostle Paul, Chapter 13, Verses 1-3

Let every soul be subject unto the higher powers. For there is no power but of God: the powers that be are ordained of God.

Her interest in Apostle Paul had waxed and waned over the years of Bible study. Today she didn't want to deal with the confusion and irritation his teachings aroused in her. But she sighed and picked up

　　　　　　　　　　　LEILA RYLAND SWAIN

her pen and began to make notes. *What do you think the verse means? How are we to understand "the powers that be?"* She still wrote in the beautiful cursive script taught in elementary school, back before the schools were filled with Black children, when many standards went out the window. In 1962 the "powers that be" had ruled separate but equal was no longer the law of the land, so in 1972 when the Supreme Court decision was finally enforced in Georgia, in her first grade in school, her classes were "diverse." Melanie said this was the proper term to use now. Dorothy told her daughter that her classes consisted of her white friends plus a few Black boys and girls. What she didn't tell Melanie was that it all seemed so strange, alien, unsettling. And that she didn't like it, then and now. The "powers that be" now seemed to her to be headed more in the right direction under the new President.

Born into the Cooper family, Doro believed she fell a notch socially when she married John Rutledge. As the owner of the thriving Chevrolet dealership, John had provided well for the family and for her financial security, she had to give him that, even though she felt embarrassed by his shirt with a gold embroidered car logo on the pocket. She wouldn't let him wear it to the Country Club. She asked John to call her Doro instead of Dorothy (a name that reminded her of Judy Garland) when she read about Poppy Bush's daughter, Dorothy whom they called Doro, and she then loved her name.

The Cooper family had sunk its roots in Gordon County, Georgia, in the 18th Century when two Scots-Irish brothers emigrated from Ireland. Being able to cite ancestors six generations back in time gave the small town family a decided luster. John's family descended from the poor English debtors General Oglethorpe brought over to found the town of Savannah, which was not a heritage to gloat over. When Melanie made fun of her pride in her ancestors, Doro got huffy and reminded her that she came from "good stock," which gave her many advantages.

"Yes, and it also gave me a huge dose of white privilege. You know, being smug about how much better we whites are than those Blacks who were brought over from Africa to serve us."

"I never said or thought that, Melanie! Why, I have always been considerate of Alice, who's been with me for ten years now, and all the women who took care of you when you were little. How can you say such a thing?"

"Because it's true."

Doro sighed as she remembered this conversation with her only child, who seemed now to want to reject every benefit she had been given, and Doro allowed herself a few moments of righteous self-pity. What if she had just let her daughter get pregnant by that boy, that Black boy she hung out with in eleventh grade and no doubt slept with, and had not put a stop to it? And worse, what if a baby was born in her family with brown skin? What if she and John had not sent her off to Emory, the best college in the South, her own alma mater, and kept her away from New York and the art school she had a half-baked desire for? And now, what if she gave Melanie her inheritance and thus enabled her to lead a life of leisure and neglect her career as a photographer? No, it was best to ignore her frequent requests for money, it would build her character. She thought she would send a nice check for her birthday in October.

She closed her notebook and tried to put the questions about the powers-that-be out of her mind. She went outside through the patio door and in the twilight she toured her small garden, glad of the rain shower in the afternoon that meant she didn't have to water. She plucked dead leaves from the dahlias and touched a finger to the Naked Ladies, those luscious pink lilies that sprang up a week ago in the hot July days. An involuntary shiver rippled up her arms as she looked at the bare blossoms, so exposed and vulnerable. She fought the image of her wedding night and her naked pink flesh laid bare to seeking hands. Ripe, decaying magnolias perfumed the air with their decadent scent and in the edge of the woods she heard a whippoorwill sound its plaintiff call. She noted in recent years how the whippoorwills were heard less and less often, and wondered briefly as to the cause.

She paused beside the sprawling crape myrtle bush John had planted a few years before his death. Her mother-in-law had gone to some progressive camp up in the mountains and had instilled some unfortunate ideas in her husband's head. He had sided with Melanie

    LEILA RYLAND SWAIN

and against her wishes, usually, but she kept the upper hand and had her way. Doro didn't feel guilty about how she achieved that because her duty was to hold to standards that were the family's only bulwark against decay and destruction. Outside those standards lay only darkness and chaos.

Yes, Doro was comfortable with her life and her decisions. And she wished to remain so, and not be confronted with radical ideas that would change her well-being and destroy her peace, She switched on the TV as she ate the dinner Alice had fixed for her earlier in the day before she left for her own home. The channel was pre-set to Fox News and she picked up her knitting—a scarf for Melanie for Christmas, a new complex pattern with metallic yarn she thought was just right for her girl. Melanie had asked for one of those pink pussy hats the feminist marchers in Washington were wearing, but Doro refused to knit such a thing. She would not, could not, give any aid to those kinds of goings-on. She viewed them as scandalous and certainly not the way she expected her daughter to behave.

She relaxed as Chris Wallace came on the screen with breaking news, but then sat upright in her chair when he began to describe how a car plowed into a crowd of protesters in Charlottesville, Virginia, killing a girl. She got the story sorted out through his reporting: white nationalists had rallied and marched through the University of Virginia, carrying torches, protesting the removal of a statue of Confederate General Robert E. Lee. Counter-protestors took to the streets to resist the marchers, and a man drove a car into a crowd of those young people.

The girl he killed was named Heather Heyer, and a picture of a young face flashed onto the TV screen. A helicopter carrying two police troopers crashed, killing both. President Trump was at his golf resort in New Jersey, where he addressed the violence and condemned "an egregious display of hatred, bigotry and violence on many sides."

Doro sat, frozen, through this searing broadcast of horror. She knew the invasion would soon be here, in her town, where a Confederate soldier on a rearing horse brandished his sword in the public park. They would tear it down, and would tear down her carefully composed life. She turned off the TV and wept for her own losses, both those of the past and the ones to come. She didn't know whether her fears were for her own security or for that soldier who protected her, and perhaps they were the same.

A memory returned to her, a memory of her college days. After a frat party, her date escorted her, as belle of the Chi Phi fraternity, on the traditional hike up the backside of Stone Mountain, where images of Confederate leaders carved into the sheer cliff of granite in front reigned over the city. In the darkness, across the rocks, she saw the white caps of a gathering of Ku Klux Klansmen and a burning cross. Their leaflets were scattered in her path. She took one up and saw the image of a huge Black man in pursuit of a white woman in a flimsy garment, her hands thrown up in dismay and fear. PROTECT OUR WOMANHOOD: these words blazed out of the page. She stuck the paper in her pocket and kept it around for a long time, but now it had slipped away, she didn't know how or where.

Doro sat in silence for a half hour, and then rose to straighten the house, to "put the house to bed" as her husband used to say. She tilted the gold-framed pictures of Lee and Jackson on the wall over the fireplace to put them back to level. She had bought these in an antique store years ago during a visit to Chapel Hill, North Carolina, with John. A Georgia Tech graduate, John loved the Yellow Jacket football teams and liked to travel to the away games when he could. She recalled how Melanie had railed against these wonderful photographs: *They were traitors to the nation and yet you've made a shrine to them.* Doro shivered, wondering how she had bred such a rebel against all of her values and her ancestors' values. The Confederate army had fought honorably for her and for the institutions of the South, and her family had not owned any slaves, so she would keep the photographs in place for now.

Doro slept uneasily that night upstairs in her queen bed, walnut posts hoisting a linen canopy over her recumbent figure in a fragile cotton nightgown. She sensed she had dreamt the entire night, but only grasped to consciousness the dream she remembered upon waking. The Negro from the leaflet chased her over the rocky slopes of Stone

                    LEILA RYLAND SWAIN

Mountain, and he caught her. She screamed and cowered at his touch, but he took her gently by the hand and led her back down the slope to the ground, where he released her to her mother and father. They were waiting beside their 1975 Lincoln Continental, the family car when she was young and on which she had learned to drive.

CHAPTER EIGHTEEN

"The waiters used to wear red Cossack smocks and the china was stamped with Faberge eggs." Viktor sipped a vodka martini and smiled at the shining face of his date, whom he had persuaded to join him in a meal at the best restaurant Atlanta had to offer: Nikolai's Roof, on the 30th floor of the Hilton Hotel. "They've changed a lot here—beige has replaced the red walls and everything—but the food is still wonderful. Russian-inspired, infused with classic French cuisine by a great chef."

He encouraged Hallie to try the Moscow Mule, and she wrinkled her nose when she first tasted it. "Ginger beer? How weird." But she continued to sip it, and Viktor was pleased she seemed to like it. He felt giddy in her company even after more than a half-dozen dates. She allowed him to hold her hand when they walked on the street and had served him sweet tea with mint at the large round table by the front window in her house. She'd also invited him to church, the famous Ebenezer Baptist Church. The setting, the sermon, the serious and devout congregation, the music—especially the amazing voice of the soloist—moved him and reminded him of St. Nicholas Orthodox Church in Birmingham, where he had been an altar boy from age seven.

Viktor already knew he loved her, but the path was not clear and certainly would not be easy. So many factors impinged on his life and on her life, too, as he had begun to understand it. He knew she did not trust him yet, and he didn't blame her—for he did not really know what his next moves would be. He tried to keep those decisions at bay for now as he pursued this woman, this graceful woman who had touched his soul. The other aspects of his life were grim and he put them in another category.

                                         LEILA RYLAND SWAIN

Hallie touched his arm and Viktor jumped, his reverie broken. "Sorry, I faded off somewhere, please forgive me." He was aghast that he'd neglected her and said, "You must be hungry." As he turned to summon the waiter, he saw a group of men at the bar and the gaze of one of them was fixed steadily on him. The man raised his glass in a salute. Viktor froze. He knew that face: Slavic features, black hair hanging over his brow. Viktor looked back at Hallie, who studied the menu. With horror, Viktor realized the man, the Ashton Kutcher look-alike sitting over there, was the Russian agent who had approached him in May. His hair was longer and he did not have on the sunglasses he wore in the garden. What was his name? Oh yes, Oblomov. Anatoly Oblomov.

Viktor often took his lunch out to the Skiles Triangle on the Tech campus on the days he was teaching and enjoyed the shade of the massive old oaks. He'd been an adjunct professor in the Russian Language for Business and Technology department for two years now, and next year he would be co-leader of a program of site visits at Russian companies and an overnight trip to Moscow. When he had a longer stretch between classes, he would drive over to the Botanical Gardens, just a mile or so from campus. With its winding paths through flowering gardens in spring and holiday lights in winter, its beauty soothed Viktor and enlarged his appreciation of plants. The changing exhibits always took him by surprise, and he marveled at their artistic merit and ingenuity. The Chihuly glass sculptures fascinated him, and the enormous mosaiculture Earth Goddess in the Cascades Garden drew him to her. He had read the garden's brochure on how mosaiculture differed from a topiary, and how embedding thousands of annual bedding plants on an armature steel structure created the intriguing effect. The Earth Goddess was wonderful and he bowed to her power.

He often loitered to appreciate her growth of plant hair and clothing, and one day in May when he leaned on the railing surrounding her lair, he realized he was not alone.

"She is quite remarkable, no?" The man leaned on the railing next to Viktor and stared at the Earth Goddess. "May I introduce myself to you, Viktor?"

That the man knew his name startled Viktor and he turned to look. The man continued: "I am Anatoly Oblomov, and a friend of your brother's." Oblomov spoke in a courteous manner, in a voice with inflections indicating his English to be a second language. The information he gave, conveyed in undertones of steely intention, frightened Viktor, who had not spoken to his older brother in many years. "Do not be alarmed, your brother is fine—for now."

These ominous words deepened Viktor's fears, but he managed to ask, "What do you want?" Viktor had only the vaguest memories of his brother, who had been left in Chechnya when his mother and father fled to America after the disintegration of the Soviet Union. Viktor was two years old. Alexander, nine years old, and his grandmother were to be sent for once the family was established, but that turned out to be impossible to carry out because of the political forces there.

Oblomov said, "Why don't we take a stroll together in this beautiful paradise?" He began walking and Viktor followed him, his heart beating fast and a bead of sweat forming on his brow. He wanted to run away back to his car, but he was curious about where this would lead and under some kind of unspoken imperative. "We know you have not been in touch with your brother Alexander in many years, and yet, he is your brother, whom you would not wish to come to any harm. Is that not so?" Oblomov took Viktor's arm and steered him down another, more deserted path through an azalea garden with massive bushes in bud. They entered an old growth forest. Viktor had been here once before and knew where they were. No other people were there now. Viktor shook his arm free, but still followed the man through the forest, and they came out at the Glade Gardens and the electric orange Chihuly tower reflected in the pool. Viktor had not come this far in the gardens before, and despite his anxiety the tower with its coiled electric wires and lights made a deep impression.

Oblomov sat down on a bench and indicated with his hand for Viktor to sit beside him. "I am not here to harm you, Viktor Durov, but to invite you to become part of a project some friends of yours in the Kremlin would like to develop here in Georgia. You are free to decline this invitation, but unfortunately for your brother Alexander

                                        LEILA RYLAND SWAIN

in Chechnya, such a decision would have consequences."

This felt surreal to Viktor, like a joke or a play being made on him. *Who was this man and what was he suggesting?*

"I don't know what you're talking about, mister, but you'd better explain yourself quickly or I'm getting up and leaving. I don't have time for games." Viktor trembled and spoke in a fierce voice to establish some mastery of the situation.

"Yes, quite right. I should explain to you. You have a tremendous opportunity to be of help to us in the next elections here in Georgia. You see, the election of the current Secretary of State to the governorship would be most timely for us and you are in a position to ensure that happens."

"Me? Why me? What is this 'position' you are talking about?"

"You are well-informed and skilled, and have the motivation because of concern for your brother's health, to make sure only the votes for Secretary Miller will be counted in this election. The votes for his opponent need to be…discouraged."

"I know nothing of this—I want to have nothing to do with this—find someone else." Viktor's agitation grew as the implications of this encounter began to hit home.

"There is no one else on our list. We also are aware of certain debt obligations from student loans that are pressing on you that could be dealt with. And, as you may recall, your brother Alexander Durov, is involved in the Chechen rebellion and has been implicated in the 2011 bombing of Moscow's Domodedovo airport. It is possible he could be found innocent, but that is now in your hands."

Oblomov stood, smoothed his jacket, and said, "Be assured our sources will know your every move. Good day, Mr. Durov." The man strode up the path and Viktor watched him until he was out of sight. He sat on the bench and stared at the glittering orange glass tower and its reflection in the pool for a long time, turning the encounter over in his mind again and again.

When he came back to the present moment in Nikolai's Roof, he found Hallie looking at him intently. "Where did you go, Viktor?" she asked. "A profound disturbance flows through your mind."

"Forgive me, Hallie—and yes, I had a worrisome recollection, but it's gone now. Let's order our dinner. What will you have? I know the seared grouper is good, as is the beef tenderloin."

Hallie's eyes lingered on his face, which was still marked by whatever place he had been, but she ordered the grouper and let the dinner proceed with no more questions. Viktor remained present and conversed with her, but now his mind was disturbed by this reminder that he was under recruitment by the Russian to interfere with the colored vote in the upcoming election and he could not ignore this warning. A place of agony and clashing forces grew in him, and the noise of battle rose to a perilous clamor by the time he hailed a taxi and accompanied Hallie back to her house. He escorted her to her door, where he then pled a headache and kissed her cheek in farewell.

CHAPTER NINETEEN

Sunday, July 22

Walter Dobbs loved his neighborhood. He grew up near it and had now lived in a beloved Victorian style house here for 35 years and hoped to never leave. At age 72, he still liked to walk the sidewalks of West End Atlanta to get his daily exercise and admire the houses, of which he thought his was the best by far. In spring, he presided over the shy unfolding of pink dogwood blossoms, those quartered beauties that reminded some folks of the cross of Jesus. In summer, when he could endure the shroud of heat, he watched kids race the streets on their bikes, shrieking for joy. They would call out, "Hey, old man, watch our style." He laughed and remembered his youthful days on wheels, his explorations, his paper routes. He kicked and scuffled through layers of golden and red leaves as autumn piled them high. He bundled up to navigate icy paths when February swung around to greet him.

He reflected on his life so far and felt satisfied he'd done what he set out to do, retiring from Atkins and Court law firm as full partner, with his integrity known widely throughout the country. He had come up through the ranks as a civil rights lawyer and then as head of the Urban League, and as adviser to congressmen and a president. All in all, a career he was proud of.

He whistled as he strolled through his neighborhood that afternoon, his path taking him past the famous Wren's Nest, once the home of Joel Chandler Harris, now a museum. The gate was closed today, but he peeked through at the unusual house he had visited many times and once again admired the decorative woodwork of the Victorian Queen Anne style and the inviting wraparound porch. He smiled as he continued his walk, relishing the memory of how he fought to have the museum admit Black patrons, which it had prohibited until 1985.

Lord, that was over thirty years ago, but the victory was still sweet. He continued to chafe over the irony of the situation that had prevailed there for many years: only white patrons were admitted. The museum featured storytellers who entertained with Brer Rabbit and Brer Fox folk tales, which Harris had collected from the slaves on the plantation where he was born, but did not permit Black folk to enter the museum. *Incredible and thoroughly reprehensible!* He gave the sidewalk a hard tap of his walking stick to underline his feelings on the matter. White mind at work.

The Shrine of the Black Madonna was just a couple of blocks down Ralph D. Abernathy Boulevard, and Walter always gave a salute to the church that celebrated Black Jesus and his Black mother. He'd gone to a service there once. Their message that emphasized the belief in a Black savior and Madonna helped counteract the damage done by acceptance of the myth of Black inferiority. He'd read about the Black Madonna in Notre Dame Cathedral in Paris and elsewhere in Europe, and he and Madie wanted to visit the shrine to her in Einsiedeln, Switzerland, next summer. Something about that dark lady stirred his heart in unexpected ways, and he wanted to follow those promptings.

Fifteen minutes later, he arrived back at his house where his wife Madie consulted with her catering staff in her office. She'd begun this business, *New Soul Provisions*, when he was in law school, and it now had a citywide reach, offering the best Southern cooking in town. She hired thirty people to cook and serve on site while she planned, supervised, and kept the books. Walter was proud of her and stuck his head into her office to say hello, waving to the crew gathered around her table whom he knew were the chief instruments of her success because they were loyal, smart, and talented.

He was about to shut the door when Madie beckoned to him. "Henry called just after you left and wants to talk to you. He sounded strained." She looked over the top of her glasses at him and Walter could see the concern in her eyes, those brown eyes that had melted him years ago and still could convey meanings hard to decipher. He knew her deep lakes of humor as well as biting sarcasm, loving understanding and compassion, and of utter truth.

                                          LEILA RYLAND SWAIN

"Henry Perry?" Walter wanted to make sure which Henry she referred to, and he was startled when she said, "Yes." Startled because he could not remember a time when Henry, his sister's oldest son, had ever called him for any reason. Of course, Walter had been involved in his young life from birth onward, but the boy had never seemed to need him the way Henry's younger brother Jordan had. The last time he'd seen Henry was when Jordan was arrested and Margaret called him for a rescue mission. When he took Jordan home that day, the boys and their mother sat around with him in the comfortable living room and talked. As he recalled, Beko Perry was not there at that time, but no one found that unusual. The boys' father had been absent at many crucial moments, and now that Walter thought about it, was off somewhere when Henry was born. Margaret didn't seem to be perturbed about it, and always said "he's working." Walter wasn't sure what his work was at the Southern Regional Council, where he now performed adequately, but never with enough drive and skills to take over the leadership.

Walter adjourned to his study in the back of the house. Pictures taken with various illustrious persons he'd been associated with in his long career covered the walls. He brushed a speck of dust from the picture of Whitney Young, a man who had helped him with just the right information at the right time. "There's enough money here for everyone," Whitney had said of fundraising. Medgar Evers's gentle, homely face gazed out at him from eye level, always catching him up for a moment in memories of this most brilliant, impressive human being whom he was blessed to have known and worked with. *Medgar, you taught me most everything I needed to know about activism, and yes, you can kill the man but you can't kill the idea.* Walter saluted the face and the life.

Walter had placed his desk in an alcove with a view over the sweep of the back yard, where Madie tended a kitchen garden for vegetables and herbs, interwoven with flowers. The surface of the desk was mostly clear with a few stacks of papers on one side. A panel of Kente cloth from Ghana hung beside it. A memento of his trip with Madie to the West Coast of Africa five years ago, the vivid hues of the woven cloth added a bright note to the subdued tenor of the room. They had visited the ancient, mammoth fortresses and castles along the Gold Coast originally built to hold gold, ivory, and other wares. They made the tortuous descent into the dark dungeons where slavers had held Africans rounded up in the interior of the country and brought to the edge of the Atlantic Ocean to be shipped to America and other destinations. In those ill-lighted, grimy prisons, Walter and Madie wept for their ravaged kin.

Walter had it in mind to start writing a memoir. He looked forward to reevaluating his life and crafting a book engaged his thoughts more and more. But now Henry Perry intervened and he had to return Henry's call. He wondered what Henry would want from him? Money? He had contributed generously to the boy's tuition at Emory and now at law school, but maybe Henry didn't know that and had run into some financial troubles. Henry had always turned to his father, Beko, rightly so, and now maybe it was something Beko couldn't, or wouldn't, handle. Briefly, Walter had a spasm of resentment, for he knew he was being pulled into something he was skilled at doing but no longer wanted to. He had rescued Jordan, who actually was his favorite nephew, from the police and hoped Henry had not run afoul of the law in some way. Probably not, he'd been a straight arrow up to now, responsible, studious. The only weird thing he'd done was go to work as a butler for Dick Miller, the Secretary of State who was running for Governor. Why on earth did he want to do that?

Walter swirled a rotary file of contacts and found Henry's name and cell number. He couldn't remember when Henry or his sister gave it to him. Walter dialed the cell phone number and Henry answered promptly.

"What's up, Henry?"

"Something I need to talk to you about right away. It's important." An urgency in Henry's voice filled Walter with foreboding.

"I'm here the rest of the day. Why don't you come over?"

"Well—uh—I'm with my friend Blair Miller."

"Miller? Dick Miller's wife?"

"Yes."

                                        LEILA RYLAND SWAIN

"This sounds highly unusual, Henry."

"Unusual would be an understatement. We need your counsel and is there a chance you could come here? She's nervous about meeting you."

"So—I'm trying to understand why you don't want to come over here. I'm guessing she wouldn't want to come here with you—because it would not play very well in the press if she was discovered to be here, at my house. Is that right?"

"That's about the size of it, Uncle Walter. I tried to convince her it would be okay, but…"

Walter heard some chatter in the background coming through the phone, a woman's voice saying "impossible…" The voice faded, and Walter said, "Okay, then, at your house?"

"Well, actually we're at Melanie's apartment—Melanie Rutledge, the photographer, you know, she's a friend of ours—she lives in Hallie Clements' basement. You know where she lives?"

"I think so. Can it wait until tomorrow? I will be going out to a meeting and could drop by then."

"Uncle Walter, actually we've got a real hot potato in our laps and we don't know what to do with it. It has to do with the voter suppression in the coming election—remember Jordan got arrested for snooping around? Something big's happening, and we found out about it by accident. Blair's here, but she won't be here tomorrow. We need you."

Walter groaned and scratched his head, wishing this need could be directed at somebody else, not at somebody who was tired of politics and just wanted to live simply, travel, and write a memoir. But duty wrestled with impatience and resentment—duty, that sorcerer who had called him early in life and kept on singing to him to join the cause against the oppression of the people of his race. He had lashed himself to the mast at last and thought he would make it through the rest of his life without succumbing to that siren call in the straits of Scylla and Charybdis. But here it was again. In spite of his professed wish to eke out his life in a serene retirement, he felt a surge of interest, excitement of a kind he thought he had put away for good.

"It's almost noon. I will have a bite to eat here, and then head over your way. Send the address to my phone, please."

"Yes, sir, yes sir, we'll be here and see you around two?" "Solid."

Walter punched his phone to end the call, and sat for a few minutes looking at the Kente cloth and remembering the slave-holding dungeons in Ghana. *There's always more to do. racism never ends.* He sighed, and rose to go and have some of his wife's good food in the kitchen and tell her he was going out. He thought he had smelled fried okra earlier and hoped Madie had saved some for his lunch. He was sure he would need to be fortified for what could become a major political upheaval in the state, in his life, and in those close to him.

CHAPTER TWENTY

Hallie had spent Saturday morning at Hair Loft Atlanta. She'd been dissatisfied with her hair for a while and wanted something different. Or so she thought. She'd not been to this salon before, but colleagues at the college bragged about it and she liked what they'd done with her assistant's hair. Hallie had worn a large Afro for years—natural hair, partially protest-based in reaction to the pervasive chemically treated Black hair—and then had switched to braids. She'd often considered dreads, but thought they would take more time than she wanted to spend creating and caring for them. Black hair had become so politicized lately—some girls had been expelled from the elementary school nearby for wearing dreadlocks, and she'd heard that law firms downtown wouldn't hire women or men with dreads. The braids had served her well for a few years, but now, she wanted something new, something softer. And then there was Viktor.

Was her hair distress about pleasing a man? She put on a stern face in the mirror and said "No," but she knew she fooled herself.

The evening with him last week aroused conflicting emotions. During a lovely dinner at one of Atlanta's finest restaurants, no escort could have been more courteous and obviously smitten. His presence appealed to her and aroused body feelings she thought she had put away long ago. She found his baldness oddly appealing—it lent a sort of strong man aura, even though so far she'd found him gentle. He'd touched her heart in the way he smiled at the children at the next table who squirmed and goaded each other to mischief, and the way he stopped to pet a stray cat on the street, whispering to it in a secret language. When he took her hand as they walked and when he gave her a sweet kiss on the lips at her door, she was almost won.

What Viktor found in her to love was not clear, she would have to know more about that. She'd read some Russian literature—mostly Chekov and Dostoevsky—which introduced her to the fervor and brooding of the Russian soul and made her think he found some resonance with her in that vein. But then again, she could be projecting such a notion onto him. Deeper conversations needed to begin, and she relished the thought of this in their next meetings. She didn't want just pillow talk, although that, too, could be delightful.

But an ominous cloud hung over the evening when his attention vanished into some private space that left him remote and cold. He didn't tell her where he'd been, and she didn't ask, but she suspected something was not right about his reverie and his inner recollections. Call it her sixth sense, her intuition, her astute grasp of human nature, and of men who had courted her. She had enjoyed the attention of a number of men so far, including her ex-husband who had turned out to be alcoholic and unfaithful.

She learned so much in the sorting out of that relationship and the discovery, after his death of cirrhosis of the liver, that he was a rich man who hid his wealth from her. He'd also obscured other aspects of his life, such as a white wife in Alabama, where he often went on "business." He had been a charmer, however. She had mostly forgiven herself for succumbing to his seduction, but had learned a hard lesson about trust. She wouldn't make that mistake again. However, she did have the house, free and clear, which she loved, and she would have suffered enormously had she lost it.

Hair Loft Atlanta had smelled delicious and teemed with the pleasant activity of women who tended the hair. Hallie looked at pictures around the walls of different hair styles—thin braids piled into an imposing crown, dreads in intricate designs, and sleek, shining bobs carved high at the nape of the neck. Those bobs impressed her, they were so delicate and soft as the locks curved around the model's cheeks. The young woman in whose chair she was directed to sit swung a blue drape around Hallie's shoulders and said, "So what's your pick today? I saw you looking at the silk press cuts. They're nice."

Hallie capitulated to the girl's endorsement and an hour or so of washing and conditioning ensued, followed by a long session with

                                        LEILA RYLAND SWAIN

a titanium hot press. The procedures relaxed her for the most part, except that as the hair began to curl around her cheeks, anxiety stabbed her. *My God, am I conforming, am I trying to alter myself to please a man?* But the thoughts passed and she walked out of the shop feeling ten years younger and fragrant. She walked home in a dreamy state, wondering how it was that the new hairdo could bring about a rising lust in her bones. A lust tempered by the danger zones popping up in her mind, as trepidation about this new possibility with Viktor mixed with excitement about what could come to pass.

The next day, Sunday, Hallie went for a walk after church, chatted with a few neighbors, and stopped at the neighborhood grocery. She walked home along Auburn Avenue and as she drew closer to her house, she saw a black limousine parked a few spaces down from her front steps. A uniformed driver leaned against it smoking a cigarette. She wondered what important person was visiting her neighborhood, she didn't recognize the car or driver. She turned and mounted her steps and as she passed the steps to the basement apartment she saw, through the window, several people gathered at the table in the front room. No one was distinct, the forms were shadowy and she suspected Melanie was entertaining some friends. She didn't make a connection between the limousine and the party in the apartment in the basement.

Hallie busied herself making beef and barley soup for dinner and cookies for a meeting at the college the next day. She bustled back and forth in her kitchen, which was in the back of the house. She glanced now and then in a mirror to see if her new hairdo still was something she wanted to stay with, she was not sure. Certainly it was different and maybe too much of a change, maybe shocking to some friends— maybe to Viktor? But what did she really know about him and his preferences and desires—and did they matter anyway? Back and forth in her mind as she debated her own stance.

After the soup was simmering and the oatmeal and raisin cookies were baking in the oven, she went to the living room to sit down for a while and read. She wanted music and went over to the radio in the corner to see what station she could find that suited her mood. Through an air duct there behind the radio, she heard voices coming up from the apartment. She recognized Henry's voice, which rose and fell in a rather long soliloquy, she could only catch parts of the words. *Voter suppression* and *do something* seemed to be what he was saying, and she figured they were having a political discussion. She wasn't sure who else was there with Henry—and Melanie she presumed—and she was not particularly interested in the conversation. Same old, same old. She was tired of politics and the possibilities of romance consumed her right now, body and soul.

Just as she found the right station, she froze. A name was spoken from downstairs.

Spoken with emphasis, it came through the duct loud and clear. *Viktor.* Surely she misheard, or it was some other person with that name. But it came again, this time in a woman's voice: *Viktor Durov.* Unmistakable. Anxiety coursed through her body. Why would they be talking about Viktor? She sorted through her knowledge of who knew him, and remembered that he had asked her about Melanie's picture—she had taken a picture of him at the lynching museum in Montgomery, and he'd found it in *Atlanta* magazine. So maybe Melanie had met Viktor somewhere, or he had sought her out.

Still, she stood by the air duct, straining her ears to try to follow the conversation going on downstairs. She heard a deep male voice, it was not Henry's voice. What other male would be there—and then she recognized the voice, although she hadn't heard it in some time. Walter Dobbs, her friend Margaret's brother and powerful civil rights activist, his resonant voice was unmistakable. And he was asking questions about Viktor Durov! Hallie covered her ears with her hands to drown out the sound of his voice—something terribly wrong in his voice—it assailed her with the force of a high wind and she trembled violently.

When she recovered and bent to listen again, she heard another voice—a woman's voice, not Melanie's. Who was that? She heard the woman say, "my husband," and she heard no more for several moments. Someone moving around. Glasses clinking on the table. Then she heard Henry's voice, insistent, certain, forceful. And he was saying, *We have to stop Viktor Durov.*

Hallie backed away from the air duct and stumbled back to the

      LEILA RYLAND SWAIN

kitchen. She was not sure that she wouldn't faint, so she sat down in a wooden chair at the table and put her head on her knees. Gradually the trembling quieted and she sat up. The timer for the baking cookies rang and she got up to take the pan out of the oven. She took the spatula and placed each cookie on a big plate to cool, finding comfort in the deliberate movements she made. An idea took hold in her mind: take cookies to Melanie in her apartment. Yes. That's what she must do, and quickly before the gathered people dispersed. She must find out what they were talking about, what they were saying about Viktor Durov.

She passed a mirror in the hall and her hands went to her hair. Her hair! Now was not the time to introduce a new hairdo, but did she have time to wash the silk out and rebraid her hair? No, the people in Melanie's apartment might disperse by the time she did that, so she'd have to go like this. She put the plate of cookies down on a table and tucked the ends of her hair curving around her cheeks behind her ears. She dreaded what she was probably going to discover in the basement, and feared the clarity she needed might come at a huge price. She ate one of the cookies to give her courage to go.

CHAPTER TWENTY-ONE

The U. S. Post Office priority mail envelope arrived at Viktor's apartment mid-morning on Sunday. He slept late after an hour of wakefulness in the middle of the night, during which he tossed and turned. He tried to interrupt the cycle of restless thoughts with breathing and meditation. Around nine, after making a pot of coffee and flicking through the TV news channels, he heard the mail slot in his front door click open and the whistling tune of the mail carrier. In slid a couple of letters, a Russian journal in plastic wrap, and the Post Office envelope, which was just slim enough to make it through the opening. The outer flap clanked shut, and Viktor regarded the pouch as if it were a copperhead unloose on the floor. He knew what the contents were as if he had x-ray vision, and the coffee curdled in his stomach.

Anatoly Oblomov had stared at him at the restaurant, and his message lurked in that package on the floor. The hard cold facts now lay in front of him and decisions were inescapable, even as they were impossible. Oblomov—what a strange name for a modern Russian to have. Viktor seized on that train of thought even as he knew it was a diversion from what confronted him. He had read the novel *Oblomov*, by Ivan Goncharov, when he was in high school in Birmingham, it wasn't assigned by the school, but the book was on his father's shelf. He took it down to read on a rainy Saturday afternoon and now remembered how the story pulled him in. After he finished it, he talked with his father about the book and the concept of "Oblomovism." The fictional Oblomov could not get out of bed, and Viktor's father, who had studied Russian literature, told him the novel was a satire of the Russian intelligentsia.

Viktor laughed to himself as he compared the Russian who had tasked him with interfering in the Georgia gubernatorial election to the fictional character. Maybe it was not his real name—maybe it was a disguise, a symbolic ruse of some kind. But what? Russians could be tricky, deceptive, maddening. They loved secret and sly jokes. A glance at the package lying on the floor brought him back to the reality of the choices he faced. This was no laughing matter at all.

But why had he been chosen for this task? He didn't remember his brother Alexander at all, for he was seven years older when the family fled Russia and Alexander was left with his babushka. Was he now to be his brother's keeper because Alexander had carried out revolutionary actions? He, Viktor, was peaceful and just wanted an ordinary life here in his adopted country. He was a citizen, a professor, and loved his family, and did not know this brother who got him into this mess. Viktor buried his face in his hands, and his heart raced in his chest—was this a heart attack? He got up and opened the refrigerator and poured a glass of water from the jug with a Brita filter. He drank it down and then began to sweat. He never sweated, but his shirt was damp and drops rolled down the side of his face.

Viktor pulled the blood pressure monitor out of the drawer of his bedside table. One twenty over eighty. Normal. But his head spun and his breathing became ragged. Did he need to call 911? Instead, he lay down on the floor in the living room, where he felt his head would blow off with the mounting anxiety. In a while, after much suffering, a filament of reason threaded its way into his mind and he breathed more easily and his body cooled and relaxed.

Viktor lay inert on the floor, awaiting his fate. He closed his eyes and fell into a reverie of tousled memories and drifting feelings. *Soft fabric brushed his face, the sleeve of his mother's gown when she kissed him good night. Her perfume in his nose, gentle words of comfort flowing through his mind. She floated there, holding him in her tender manner, assuring him of her love. Her face hovered, disembodied, calling him home, calling him to her side, a porcelain face, aristocratic, proud, intelligent. Her sweet voice murmured a story again as she had always done by his bedside. The story was of Vasilisa, an orphan child sent to fetch light. Her dying mother had given her a doll that would always protect her. She encountered the dread Baba Yaga, the fearful witch. To get the light, Vasilisa had to perform impossible tasks, but the doll in her pocket completed them all.*

Navigating a slow return to sensibility took Viktor an hour. He lay on the floor flexing his arms and feet. Turning his head he could see the offending package lying by the door and he knew the contents, so that was not a question. Who sent it, he knew that as well. His mind clouded over when he came to the next question: what was he to do? An ancient, creaking rack pulled him apart in exquisite torture, hands one way, feet another, the wheel grinding as he didn't answer the question in a manner satisfactory to a masked interlocutor. Despair settled in, a dull throb of agony, a lifetime fate of indecision, humiliation, depression. Baba Yaga was having her sport with him.

A miraculous light arose within. The doll in Vasilisa's pocket protected her. Viktor turned on his side, thinking of the doll, and he saw the present his mother had sent him for Christmas. The colorful red garment of the *matryoshka* doll in her long *sarafan* garment winked at him from the shelf where he had placed her just last week.

He dragged himself over to the shelf and brought the doll down to rest on the floor within his crossed legs. Her painted eyes regarded him peacefully from under her babushka and her presence soothed his mind. His mother had sent a note explaining that she brought this doll from Russia when they emigrated, that it was old and nothing like the mass produced dolls tourists bought at the airport duty-free shops. He opened the first doll into two halves and encountered another dressed in similar clothes, but with different vivid colors. On and on, through the dolls, until he reached the tiniest one, who was not cut in half. She was whole, with a blue headscarf, and felt steady in his palm. He put her in his pocket, felt her tremble and then fall still.

   LEILA RYLAND SWAIN

CHAPTER TWENTY-TWO

Dick Miller, clad only in a tattered red plaid bathrobe, planted his hairy legs with bulging calves in front of the liquor cabinet, and shook a few drops out of the Noah's Mill bourbon bottle. Damn. Empty. Where did it go? Was Blair, or the cleaning people for god's sake, nipping at his good stuff on the sly? No, Dick had to admit he had drunk it, all of it, by himself in just three nights. He reached back on the shelf and dragged out a bottle of Early Times, to which he turned only in emergencies such as this. That was what he drank back in Waycross in his youth. He needed to drown out ever-increasing worries about the upcoming election—and about Blair. Especially about Blair. Like, where the hell was she all afternoon?

The morning had been uneventful, just the newspaper and coffee and conversation—what did they talk about? Oh, yes, he had told her that he was going on a trip with Viktor Durov. Her face blanched and her coffee cup rattled as she put it in the saucer. What was that about? He thought she liked Viktor, and he'd even felt a little jealous of him, thought he'd made eyes at her several times.

"What's the matter?" Dick had steadied her cup so it didn't tip over and frowned at her.

"Where are you and Viktor going?" Blair's voice was thin, unsteady, unlike her usual mellow tone. She looked at him in a manner he had not seen in her before—fierce, like a tiger coiled in the shade, ready to spring. He imagined fangs sinking into his hand and shook his head to clear the image.

"We're going up to Kennesaw to the election center there. Just want to make sure everything's copacetic for the election. Viktor's helping us with that."

"You're going today?" Blair had become steely quiet, sitting like a stone on her chair.

"No. We have an appointment Wednesday afternoon."

Blair got up, cleared the breakfast dishes, and left the room. He had heard her mount the stairs and go into the bedroom. Then he had heard her talking to someone on her cell phone, he would have listened in if she'd used the house phone. The grandfather clock in the dining room struck eleven as she came back in the kitchen dressed in black jeans, a thin black blouse he'd never seen before, and her pink Nike running shoes, the ones he had once thrown in the garbage. He had told her not to get such expensive sneakers, but she had ignored him. She had grabbed the keys to the Porsche off the hook by the back door, and was out the door without another word.

"Where are you going?" he had yelled as he ran out to the back stoop, but she backed the car around and took off down the driveway toward West Paces Ferry Road. "Damn it, Blair, come back here now." His ineffectual cry boomed out over the backyard and faded into the shrubbery, startling only the downy woodpeckers hanging on the suet cake in the bird feeder. Dick banged the door, catching his index finger in the flap. He hopped around the kitchen sucking his finger and uttering curses to the sink and the refrigerator.

At six o'clock, Dick had two shots of neat bourbon, felt dizzy, and lay down on the living room carpet and ruminated. The grandfather clock struck seven. Seven o'clock in the evening? Dick didn't believe it, and punched the Fitbit on his left wrist, but the digital time display confirmed it. Where had the day gone? He sat up fast when he heard the car coming up the driveway and shook his head to clear it. Was that Blair? He levered himself up to standing and swayed as he marched to the back door. Yes, that was his wife getting out of the car. He was momentarily relieved, but then rage swelled in his throat and he smashed his fist into the wall beside the door. Pieces of drywall broke off under the impact and fell on the floor. Blood streamed from his knuckles as he hit the wall again and again, screaming.

***

                                                 LEILA RYLAND SWAIN

Melanie's cell phone rang at eight o'clock in the evening, but she didn't pick up. Everyone left her apartment around six and she had scarfed down leftover Pad Thai carryout from the refrigerator. She collapsed on the sofa under the weighted blanket she'd found at her favorite thrift shop on Ponce de Leon Avenue. She stroked the soft fabric of the blanket and marveled at finding such an item with the sale tags from Macy's still attached. One of the rich ladies from the mansions nearby with too much money and too little sense apparently didn't like to be weighted any more than she already was. The blue floral pattern pleased Melanie's eye and she relaxed into comfort under the gentle pressure on her body. Warm and content, she decided to ignore the phone call and cuddle a bit longer and let the stress of the meeting that afternoon recede, stress accompanied by excited determination on the part of the participants. She was ready to do her part, but now a nap claimed her.

Melanie awoke at ten, pushed the blanket off, and sat up on the couch, yawning and rubbing her eyes. Her cell phone on the coffee table blinked. She drank from her water bottle, went to the bathroom, and then picked up the phone to hear the message someone left. She heard the voice of her mother.. *Hi honey, guess what? I'm in Atlanta! My friend Alison—you remember her—wanted a companion for a brief trip and so I said yes. Exciting for this stay-at-home. We're at the Waldorf Astoria Buckhead, and I want to take you shopping.. Okay? Let's meet tomorrow at ten at Lenox Square. Call me back. Love you.*

Melanie grimaced. "Ugh, no." She deleted the message and sank back on the sofa, clutching the weighted blanket. A memory of her childhood yellow blankie came to her, her blankie she had clung to for years, didn't want washed, it took away the smell that comforted her. Her mother would often hide the blankie and lecture her about "being too big now to drag around this childish thing." Doro never actually threw it away but each time it vanished Melanie screamed and couldn't sleep. She cried endlessly until her mother pulled it out of hiding and threw it at her.

Now, Melanie shivered as she recalled the battles over clothes that came later when she wanted to wear khaki pants from the Army surplus store and t-shirts emblazoned with Eminem and Madonna. Doro fought her endlessly over what was appropriate to wear to school: a knee-length skirt, a frilly cotton blouse, and a pastel sweater with a circle pin attached at the neck. "In what dark age did you come into being, Mom? I wouldn't be caught dead in that sixties' crap."

Yes, Melanie had railed against the clothes her mother picked out, but had to wear them when her usually-reliable father sided with Doro. Now father was gone, but Doro never gave up and still wanted to "dress her" again. Be damned if she would comply. But a new thought arose in Melanie's mind. She did need new clothes, and she had no money to buy them.

The plan they had hatched this afternoon would require her to dress more formally than her usual pants and t-shirts. Maybe she could maneuver her mother into buying the right outfit for her. Certainly worth a try. She sprang to the phone, dialed her mother's number, and agreed to meet her at the NM Café in Neiman-Marcus at the mall at noon tomorrow. Doro would be good for lunch, too. Melanie hoped her mother wasn't stuck on the idea of frills and furbelows like something out of *Southern Living* magazine as she often was in the past. Melanie's task called for an outfit like a partner in a downtown law firm crossed with a lady of the night at Tenth and Peachtree. Something molding to her body in a chic sort of way, designed to garner the briefest of gaze by the men masquerading in suits and ties. Doro would go for it like a bee for the flower or the goat for the privet hedge. Or the Republicans for power.

***

Henry left Tamila's bed at four a.m., slipping down to the kitchen and out the back door. No one else in the household was up yet. Tamila turned over and slept for another hour and a half, then roused herself to make coffee and consider that Henry had proposed to her last night. Would he remember this in the broad daylight? She wondered about his constancy, and if she was ready to marry him. She laughed as she poured the coffee, now she had the upper hand and she could dangle him along, if she wanted to.

But the more important thing was what Henry had told her about plans afoot at the Capitol and she wanted to dress up. Since she'd been going down to the office where she was interning, she'd tried to dress better than her student jeans and t-shirt. She adopted black as her staple color and with the stipend and birthday money from her mother she had gone shopping. She looked at, and rejected, every dress on the rack at PinkSky Boutique, so she decided to brave Neiman-Marcus. She had never been in that store before, she'd felt intimidated by the aloof sales people with tight, sleek chignons, but felt pleased that she sailed right through, nodding to these ladies. She might be a bride! And she could shop for her wedding dress here—if she had a wedding.

With the help of one of the snooty ladies, she found an impeccable black wool-blend jacket she couldn't resist. The woman actually was friendly and said, "You'll wear this everywhere." She gasped at the price, but had saved up. And it felt good. She paired the jacket with an ivory cowl-necked camisole she borrowed from her sister and her old black skirt. She had to wear the black pumps, but the heels were high enough to speak fashion. She wanted to speak fashion and see if her boss, Dick Miller, noticed. Yes, that was her agenda today: to garner the Secretary of State's attention. And then she would pounce.

Henry had told her that Secretary Miller was going to travel up to Kennesaw State University on Wednesday with Viktor Durov. Their mission, according to the grapevine (which is what Henry called his source), was to fiddle with the voting apparatus located there, which served the entire state. Henry described it as a nefarious agenda, part of the plot to suppress the vote in the next election. In all likelihood, Miller would come to the office first and then meet with Durov, and they would drive together up I-75 to Kennesaw. If Tamila played her cards right, she would be with them.

***

Henry trudged down to campus to torts class that day full of worry. He had not told Tamila another person would also be on that trip.

He didn't inform her that Melanie Rutledge, representing *Atlanta* magazine as their official photographer, would be on the trip and that the editor of the magazine had called in a personal favor from Dick Miller for her presence. He knew if he had been totally transparent, Tamila might not have been so loving as she was, and she had given herself to him completely. His mind drifted back to her sweet kisses and excited cries, which he had to hush. She had giggled and said no one could hear and wouldn't care if they did. Admittedly, he was prudish, and she might push him past some of that. Yes!

He cringed because if he'd told her about Melanie, she might have thrown him out of the house. He listened to the drone of the professor and the rustling papers and shifting feet of his fellow students, fully aware of how he traded long term trust for short term gain. His head hurt. What good would an understanding of torts be if he lost her love?

He had walked Uncle Walter to his car after the meeting ended at five o'clock. The driver sprang to open the door for his boss.

"Give you a ride home, Henry?" Walter asked as he prepared to slide into the back seat.

"That's okay, Uncle Walter, I need to walk and organize my thoughts, but thanks."

"Tell your mother hello and…what can I say? You'll do well, I'm sure, and I've always got your back."

"Right. See you later." Henry watched the car move down the street; he could see Walter's shiny head through the back window, bending toward the driver with some instruction. Henry wondered where he was going, if not to his home, then where? A new respect for his uncle had taken hold in Henry's mind, the man was old—what, in his seventies now? But he knew what the hell he was talking about. Henry knew he had always pushed his uncle's help away, relying on his father Beko, but now he could see the differences in the men in a new light.

He saw more of his mother in Walter, and, duh, they were siblings of course. The practical wisdom, the acceptance of the way things were, but the drive to make them better as well—these were Dobbs traits.

The Perry gene of his father was more laid-back, humorous, let

     LEILA RYLAND SWAIN

sleeping dogs lie kind of heritage. Maybe it was that his dad grew up in poverty in South Georgia, and Walter grew up here in the city in a solid middle-class family. Henry thought that might have an influence on their characters, but he couldn't parse it further at the moment. More and more, Henry recognized the dual features in his own character, seeing his drive to become an attorney from the Dobbs line and his willingness to be a butler from Perry traits. He'd settled the butler debacle, but wanted to find ways to give more play to his Beko traits without submitting to debasement at the hands of whites.

The way the old man handled Melanie and Blair knocked Henry off his chair, and he witnessed the girls listening to Walter in a way he had not seen in them before. They were in awe, and he treated them gently but didn't mince his words.

Rain had washed the streets clean while they had talked in Melanie's apartment. The asphalt glistened with small puddles, and a slight breeze wove freshness through the air. July in Atlanta could still spread glory around once in a while as far as Henry was concerned. He ambled down the street, not sure where he was headed at the moment, but content in a new way and charged with energy. Melanie had emerged during the afternoon as different from how he had known her before—it was like a sudden battery connected in her personality, and she was all business and ready to do her part. Her photography skills would stand her in good stead as she took on the delicate matter of getting Viktor Durov in a compromising position.

And Blair Miller! My God, she was literally soaking in the new understandings Uncle Walter led her to with his brilliant short lectures on voter suppression and what the Republicans would not stop at to retain power and control. Money and power—that's what they were all about. She teetered on the edge of loyalty to her husband and the cut of the truth being spoken in that room. Henry could reach no conclusion in his mind as to how that would turn out. Blair's character and resolve lay on the balance scales and created worry in his mind as to whether she was going to be able to do her part with her husband.

Absorbed in thought, Henry was barely conscious of his feet on the sidewalk and the traffic passing by him in the street. When he became aware of how dark the evening had become, he found himself in front of Tamila's house. Of course. His heart swelled in his chest for he knew then he headed there from an inner guidance not yet fully revealed, a knowing that here lay his future and his healing. He hoped Tamila still loved him and had forgiven him. He was fairly certain she would be eager to play her part in the drama about to unfold.

CHAPTER TWENTY-THREE

Wednesday, July 25

The limousine wove expertly in and out of traffic on I-75 going north and the skyline of Atlanta, spiked by sunlight, glimmered in the rear window. Tamila sat on the fold-down seat facing backwards and she realized she'd never seen that view before. She'd lived all her life so far in Atlanta but had not looked at it from the outside. She didn't know the names of the buildings rising high in the sky, but they impressed her. She wanted to see them at night, see how they lit up, if they did.

Mr. Durov was sitting next to her and saw her gaze. "The tallest one is the Bank of America Plaza. It's beautiful at night." Tamila looked at him. Can he read my mind? His bald head gleamed in the light streaming through the sunroof, and she thought he looked harmless, even pleasant. He smelled fresh, like some expensive after-shave lotion. Where was the evil Russian monster Henry had depicted? She noticed he kept his hand in his suit coat pocket, fingering some object she could not see or make out what it was.

Her boss sat opposite Durov but seemed to be unconcerned with him or anyone. His black hair sprang up from his forehead in a weird cowlick she'd never noticed before, and his suit was wrinkled. He looked rumpled and had a five o'clock shadow. Tamila wondered what was the matter, she had never seen him less than impeccably dressed and shaved. Since that night at the church when he had run out of gas and shouted during her singing, he had been sweet to her. He continually stared at her while she moved around the office and said, "Looking good today, Tammy." He couldn't, or refused to, say Tamila. Just a beach too far for him, she guessed.

And then there was that girl, Melanie. Just after she and Mr. Miller and Mr. Durov had settled in the car, Melanie showed up. She tapped along the sidewalk in high heels and opened the front passenger door. "Hi everybody!" she called out in a fake cheerful voice. "I'm on assignment from *Atlanta* Magazine and have permission to ride up to Kennesaw with you."

"What the hell?" Mr. Miller growled from the back seat. But she was already seated and fastening her seat belt. The driver looked over his shoulder at Mr. Miller, but his head was bent over some papers so the driver took that as an assent and pulled the car into the driveway and away from the building.

The car was going too fast for the Chastain Road exit and the car swerved. Viktor fell against Tamila and grasped her arm to right himself. A tiny doll in his hand fell on the floor of the car and rolled to the door. He bent to retrieve it and put his finger to his lips to signal silence to her. A flush spread over his cheeks.

Dick looked up from his papers, a scowl on his face. "What was that, Viktor?"

"Nothing, nothing at all." Viktor's tone was soothing. and Dick didn't pursue the question, but he scanned both their faces intently, as if looking for some secret guilt, some shared conspiracy between the two from which he was deviously excluded.

The limo turned left on Chastain Road, and then right on Campus Drive and headed toward the Technology Center. Students in shorts and running shoes trekked along the sidewalk in the heat. When the car stopped, Dick was the first to climb out. He beckoned to Viktor and took his arm, propelling him along to the door of the Center where a man with a shock of white hair held open the door. Melanie and Tamila climbed out and stared at each other, neither was quite sure what the other was doing there. They had met a couple of times before, briefly, and each woman was aware of, and curious about, the other. They eyed each other up and down: Tamila in her chic black jacket and Melanie in a well-fitted cerise gabardine dress and stiletto red heels, a discreet camera bag slung over her shoulder. Melanie turned and started toward the Center's door.

Tamila stuck out her tongue at her behind her back. She hated her, but hurried to catch up. She was hot in her jacket but didn't want to take it off, because her blouse was sleeveless. She didn't like her bare

                                    LEILA RYLAND SWAIN

arms. She would swelter on, although her mission to divert Secretary Miller's attention was a bust so far.

Suddenly Melanie stopped short in the walkway, and turned to Tamila. "Look, I don't know why you're here and you don't know why I'm here, but there must be a reason. Can we fight a duel some other time?" She glared at Tamila and then turned too fast and stumbled in her high heels. Tamila lurched toward her and caught her arm to steady her. Melanie smiled at her, and then they both laughed. "O Lordy, let's go in and see what's happening."

"Can I see your ID, girls?" The uniformed guard just beyond the revolving door loomed before them, blocking their way.

"We're with Secretary Miller." Melanie tried to steer Tamila past the guard, but he grabbed her arm. She screamed, "Take your hands off me," pulled out of his grasp, and continued to yell. "Secretary Miller, wait for us!"

Down the hall, Dick Miller stopped and turned when he heard her voice. "Well, come on, Melanie. Take some pictures." And to the guard he yelled, "It's okay, officer, those girls are with me." He beckoned to them and then did a piercing whistle, two fingers in his mouth, like calling his hounds. Melanie and Tamila loped down the hall, Melanie showing surprising agility in her high heels.

Miller stared at Tamila and as she drew closer, he pulled her in with an arm around her waist. "Looking good, girl," he said as he took in her new outfit and the smile pasted on her face. She smiled even though she was being called a "girl" by a man she detested, because her strategy was working. She moved along with him down the hall, while Melanie matched her step to Viktor's. He was a step or two behind Dick, head down, and a lag in his stride bespoke reluctance of some sort as Melanie approached him.

"Hi," Melanie said. Viktor looked around at her and frowned.

"I'm Melanie, the photographer, don't you recognize me?"

Viktor resumed his stare at the floor. "You're the woman who takes pictures of me and I don't know why."

"There's something mysterious about you, and I keep trying to figure it out."

"I'm a completely ordinary person, I assure you." He quickened his step and suddenly veered off to the left toward the Men's Room. "I must excuse myself." He disappeared into the bathroom.

"Damn." Melanie saw Dick at the end of the hall, pulling open a door. He turned around and saw her and waved his hand at her to come on. His hand flapped back and forth so vigorously that Melanie felt alarmed and hurried toward him. Out of the corner of her eye, she saw Viktor slip out of the bathroom and head down another corridor, out of sight. Dick grabbed her hand and pulled her toward the door, but she broke away from his grasp. "I've got to go to the Ladies Room, Dick. Be back in a minute."

She pulled her camera out of the shoulder bag and turned it on. When she came to the corridor down which Viktor had gone, she put the camera strap around her neck, peered through the lens, and adjusted the settings for the available light, keyed up the focus. She passed doors until she saw Viktor in one of the offices and pushed into the room, camera up. He was approaching a big machine and had something in his hand. Melanie started shooting as she moved toward him. His hand was moving, and she got the shot. Viktor turned around and saw her and smiled. He extended his hand and in it was a small doll with a red head scarf, red circles on its cheeks, and a red rose in the middle of her chest. He put it in Melanie's hand and she bent to look at it. Viktor moved beside her and, hiding his other hand behind his hip, pushed a flash drive into a slot. It flashed a blue light to indicate it was working.

"Yes, Melanie," Viktor said, turning to her, "it's my totem doll. Do you like her?'

   LEILA RYLAND SWAIN

CHAPTER TWENTY-FOUR

Thursday, July 26

When Mrs. Murphy, the housekeeper, let herself in through the back door the next morning, she heard the quiet hum of the refrigerator and felt cool air blowing through the ducts in the floor. She put her coat and purse in the closet and when she turned around, she saw red drops on the floor. She wiped them with a paper towel and held it to her nose. Blood. She saw the damaged wall by the door and wondered what had gone on here.

She took out the hose to the central vacuum system and moved into the living room. Mrs. Miller was lying on the sofa, one hand dangling over the edge. She called out, "Mrs. Miller?" Blair's eyes opened and she turned her head to look at the housekeeper. Mrs. Murphy rushed to her side and dropped to her knees on the carpet, taking up Blair's arm and feeling for her pulse.

"I'm okay." Blair's voice was weak, but she shifted her body to lie on her side and squeezed Mrs. Murphy's hand. She wore a sleeveless nightgown and her feet were bare. Bruises on her arms and neck were an ugly red and she had a black and blue swelling around one eye. "Help me get up." Blair raised her torso and leaned on the older woman to sit on the side of the sofa. "Could you fix me some coffee and eggs and toast?"

"Of course, but should I call the doctor?"

"No, I'll be okay as soon as I eat something. I'm going to get dressed and come down to the kitchen to eat, okay?" Blair pushed off the sofa and managed to climb the steps to the upstairs. Mrs. Murphy went to the kitchen and rummaged in the refrigerator for eggs and bread.

When Blair came down to the kitchen, she had showered and dressed in skinny blue jeans and lace up boots and an indigo turtleneck tunic was pulled up to her chin. She had put makeup on the bruises and curled her hair around her face to hide them. She rolled a leather travel bag on wheels behind her and parked it at the back door.

Blair scraped up every bit of the scrambled eggs and slathered strawberry jam on the toasted sourdough bread and asked for another cup of coffee. The kitchen grew warm with the sun shining through the casement windows, stroking the table and tendrils of Blair's blond hair with light. She pushed back from the table and called to Mrs. Murphy, who had gone to straighten the living room where a chair had been turned over.

"Mrs. Murphy, I need you to promise you will never discuss this morning and my situation with anyone, ever—and especially not to my husband."

"Oh, Mrs. Miller, I won't—but I'm worried about you, are you sure you will be safe here?"

"No. But I will be safe, because I'm leaving here. So you must keep totally silent, okay? You simply didn't see me. If you have any trouble with Mr. Miller, please call me." She gave the woman her cell phone number written on a piece of paper. "I hate to be dramatic, but please memorize this number and then burn the paper. Don't give the number to anyone."

Blair put on dark sunglasses and gave Mrs. Murphy a hug. She went out the back door to the garage, where the Porsche was parked. And then she was gone.

***

Blair looked at the mansion in the rear view mirror of the Porsche and held back the tears. She didn't want to smear the makeup she'd put on to hide the bruises around her eyes. She'd managed to fool Mrs. Murphy into thinking she was okay but now her hands trembled on the wheel and her foot slipped off the accelerator a couple of times. It was a fine day, however, and drifting leaves brushed past her windshield. Her wedding day had been a day just like this one. She had stood, triumphant, on the steps of the cathedral holding her new husband's hand with a shining, unbruised face. How innocent she had

　　　　　　　　　　　　　　　LEILA RYLAND SWAIN

been, ignoring the clues blatant to everyone else that she was in for trouble. How stupid she'd been! Why had she put up with it for so long? Why had she married him in the first place? What had attracted her to Dick Miller, avowed racist and abuser? These were answers she needed to find, answers to the questions that Walter Dobbs posed to her in the meeting in Melanie's apartment. Questions that had been haunting her..

She'd tried to be a good wife and carry out her responsibilities. Now the pain of how she'd been led astray by the expectations heaped on her from the beginning of her life spread through her body. She held the car in the road with hands tightly gripped on the steering wheel just following the road to wherever she was going. She didn't think about it at all and when she gained some perspective, she wondered where she should go. Where could she go? There was no home anymore and she was adrift, on a road, alone. Road signs flashed by and she realized she was on Highway 400 north. She must have turned near Buckhead but had no memory of it.

She'd spent many idle and satisfying hours along the Chattahoochee River, and the turn to the National Recreation Center along the river was one she'd taken many times. She navigated into the parking lot, and was finally able to stop the car and turn off the motor. She rested her head on the steering wheel, feeling dizzy and sick, but the feelings slowly passed. A picnic table where she'd often eaten a sandwich was a few yards away and she managed to drag herself to it and lie down. A massive oak tree with shining leaves shaded the table, and she slept.

When she stirred to wake, a warm body lay next to her. Reaching out, she patted soft fur and turned to encounter a red dog looking at her. It licked her hand. She cuddled with the dog, its head nestled under her chin, for a long time. It smelled clean and fresh. There had been a dog in her childhood, a friend who had long been forgotten. Rusty, he was called, and her father gave him to her as a puppy. Whatever had happened to Rusty? She sat up abruptly on the table to consider it and the dog scrambled up beside her. She could not remember, but the lightness of being she'd had playing with Rusty, sleeping with him, came back to her. Her only companion.

Then she knew. Her mother. Deidre had told her Rusty ran away. But his leash and collar were hanging on the hook in the mud room. His collar was never off him. A tide of unwanted feelings swept over her, first fiery rage and then a gloom of spirit unlike any she'd ever experienced. She couldn't lift her legs, they were cemented to the table, her head a block of wood. She stroked the dog's head and let the tears streak her makeup. To hell with vanity. She examined the dog for which he (and it was a male she could see) sat patiently, twitching his ears. There was no sign of neglect or wounds, he was well fed and muscular, although not large. From his color and build she suspected a retriever, maybe a Chesapeake Bay. Rusty had been a mutt, a lovable one, and this dog seemed to be a twin in his gentleness and composure. He had no collar and she wondered if he had a chip.

"Well, dog, what comes next? Where is your owner? I'm going to move on before dark. Do you want to come with me, and we'll try to find to whom you belong? Huh?" The dog barked. She took that as an affirmation and squirmed off the table, shaking her legs and taking a few tottering steps. The dog followed. She opened the passenger door to the Porsche and he jumped right in as if he did that every day.

She started the car, but then it struck her. Where was she to go? There was no home to return to, no husband, no child to tend. Her family home was long since gone, and she was alone. Melanie. Of course. Melanie would take her in. She sank her head on the steering wheel. No. That's the first place Dick would look for her. She would be trapped and dragged back to the house and put under lock and key. She raised her head and looked at the dog. He seemed to wink at her. Maybe she had time to get to Melanie's before Dick would be missing her. He was going on a day trip today, and wouldn't be home until late afternoon. What time was it? She looked at her watch, but there was no watch on her wrist. Damn. The sun was high overhead and so she figured it must be around noon. She had time. She roared out of the parking lot. The dog stuck his head out the window and barked at a squirrel.

Traffic on the expressway south was a snarl as usual and sweat crept down her back and under her thighs on the leather seat. She should have peed at the park and now that need was becoming urgent. The warning light on the dashboard came on indicating she was low on fuel. She decided not to exit the expressway to refuel but to depend on the Porsche having enough gas to get her to Sweet Auburn. She wove in and out of traffic and finally took the exit for Freedom Parkway and held her breath as she moved over the four lanes of traffic to turn on Boulevard. When she pulled up in front of Hallie's house, the fuel gauge stood on empty.

She let the dog out of the car and he peed discreetly by the bank in the grass and hopped up the steps behind her. There was no answer to her knock, so she peered in the front window, which was open, and called out. No one was there.

As she came up the steps from the basement apartment, Hallie opened her door and came out. "Blair? Blair, come up here," she called. "Oh my God, what's happened to you?" Hallie pulled her into her arms and held her tight, then pushed her away and looked at the tear-stained bruises around her eyes.

"Dick?"

"Yes."

"Come inside." Hallie pulled her inside and shut the door. The dog lay down on the porch and put his head on his paws.

Hallie put an ice bag on her bruised eye and settled her on the sofa with a slew of bright pillows and a cup of chamomile tea.

"Does Dick know you are here?" Hallie frowned as she sat back in her chair.

"No. He left early this morning. Someone picked him up at eight.

Hallie consulted her watch. "It's 3 o'clock.

"He will get home soon and find me not there, and the Porsche gone. I don't know what to do."

"You can't stay here. This house is the first place he will look for you. Do you have any friends he doesn't know about?"

"No, unfortunately, only Melanie—and more recently you, and Henry."

"Henry! Yes, that's it. I'll call Margaret Perry and see if she will take you in for a while."

"I don't know her—will she like me? Will Henry mind? But Dick would never look for me there. And I can figure out what to do next." Blair sat up, full of the unsettled irony that would cast her into the arms of her former butler's mother. "Oh, there's a dog outside—will they take the dog?"

***

Henry arrived at Hallie's door within fifteen minutes of the call. He escorted a wobbly Blair to the Camaro, retrieved her bag from the Porsche, and drove her and the dog to his mother's house three blocks away. He delivered Blair into the arms of his mother at the front door and took the dog to the back yard and put him in the fenced enclosure. "Sorry, buddy, you gotta stay here for now, but I'll come back and look after you soon." He refilled the water bowl with the hose. The dog bumped noses with Fetch, then settled in the shade and looked around at his new surroundings with what seemed to Henry like relief.

He carried a red gasoline can back to Hallie's house and filled the tank of the Porsche. He loved the roar of the motor and the smell of fine leather seats and the feeling of momentary pride to be behind the wheel of such a vehicle. He'd never even seen a Carrera 911 Turbo except in pictures. Miller had kept it locked in his garage. But the sense of his hurried mission loomed as he backed out carefully and headed down to the intersection. He had to hide the car. Where could he take it to make sure it would not be discovered or reported? He drove around several blocks as he debated the problem and finally thought of his friend Darrien who lived nearby on Auburn Avenue, had a large double garage with an empty side, and could be counted on to keep his mouth shut.

He and Darrien stood in the driveway admiring the car together while Henry explained the situation. Assured the car was not stolen, just in need of a hiding place for a while, Darrien agreed if he could drive it around the block once. Henry was getting nervous about the time, but felt he owed his buddy that. They made an uneventful circle around the block and Darrien backed it into the garage. Henry took

 LEILA RYLAND SWAIN

the keys and they shut the garage door. Darrien said he would explain to his parents, they would understand. Henry said they could call his mother if they needed more information. Darrien offered to drive him home in his own car, but Henry said he wanted to walk.

He headed for Hallie's house to tell her Blair was safe and that he'd hidden the Porsche. She invited him to come in but he wanted to wait for Melanie outside. He couldn't decide whether to tell her where Blair had gone. The less she knew the better for her when Dick Miller came looking for his absconded wife.

CHAPTER TWENTY-FIVE

When the driver of the government van pulled up behind his house, the first thing Dick noticed was that the garage door was open and the Porsche was gone.

"Hey!" he yelled at the driver, who was turning around and about to roar off. "My car is gone."

The driver didn't hear him, or pretended not to hear him, and took off down the driveway. The van almost shimmied in its haste.

"Come back here, you bastard! I'll have your job, you worthless scum." Dick ran a few yards after the van, but a stitch in his side slowed him down and he bent over to catch his breath. He hobbled back up the driveway and used his key to open the back door.

"Blair?" Dick called for her through the house and ran up the stairs to check the bedroom. It was empty, the bed was made, and everything was in order. He went back to the kitchen and noticed that everything was spic and span. No supper was on the stove. Then he noticed a folded piece of paper on the table. At least she left him a note.

He opened it and read it.

Dear Mr. Miller, I'm sorry but I won't be able to come to clean for you and Mrs. Miller again. My rheumatism has got so bad that I can't do it any more. Here is my key.

Mrs. Murphy

Dick ripped the note in half and threw it in the garbage can. He opened the refrigerator, which was bare except for a torn open carton of cans of diet coke. He pulled one out and sat at the table to try to calm his growing agitation. Where was Blair? The cold tart cola spread in his mouth and down his throat, making him burp, and what had happened last night slowly came back to him. The knowledge of his behavior did nothing to quash his anxiety. He glanced up and saw the gouged out drywall beside the kitchen door and the stain around it that Mrs. Murphy had tried to wipe off. His knuckles began to sting again, as they had off and on all day. God, he remembered the blood on Blair's face, she had been so stupid about the trip he made with Viktor and she wouldn't shut up. Lecturing him about voting rights. What the hell was that about? Where was she? Should he phone the hospitals? No, that would look bad.

Blair probably was at Melanie's. It's where she went the last time there was a fight and she felt hurt. She'd come around, she always did. It was a bitch now that they didn't have the Jeep any more that she used to drive, but he had to keep her from running all over town like she did, not staying home, wasting a lot of fuel.

He turned on the TV and flipped channels for a half hour and then dialed Melanie's number. No answer. He left a message. He found a rerun of season nine of The Real Housewives of Atlanta, which he secretly loved while always panning it when somebody mentioned it. Blair hated it so that made it even more a surreptitious pleasure. He particularly liked NeNe Leakes and could sometimes jack off when she strutted around. This afternoon she reminded him somehow of Tamila. My, she had looked fine today

When he looked up again, it was dark outside and Melanie had not called back. He dialed her again. She picked up on the first ring.

"Hi Dick. I haven't seen Blair."

"Well, where the hell is she? And she's taken the Porsche."

"Gee, I don't know, Dick. Is everything okay—is she okay, to your knowledge?"

"We had a little fuss last night, but nothing serious. She's fine—she just needs to come home."

"If I hear from her, I'll tell her you called."

"Okay. And tell her I don't have any transportation up here—my secretary drove me today and she let me off and the Porsche is gone."

"Don't you have a state owned car?"

"Yeah, but it's over at the Capitol. I'll have someone bring it to me."

"Okay, Dick. Gotta go now."

The line went dead. Dick stood up and stumbled over his shoes. Fuck it, the woman was lying to him. He knew it. Blair was sitting right there in Melanie's apartment, and now they were laughing about fooling him. Well, he was no fool, and he would go over there and surprise them in their little game.

Dick started to call an Uber, but then he had a better idea. A brilliant idea, actually, even if he said so himself. He dialed the number for the State Patrol in his cell phone and asked for Major Matt Humboldt, a man he'd recommended for promotion to his position of chief of the Northern Division, which included Atlanta.

"Hi Matt, Dick Miller here."

"Yes, sir, how are you? How can we help you tonight?"

"Well, Matt, my wife is missing. Yep, I got home an hour ago and both she and my Porsche were gone. She hasn't come home, and there's no answer on her cell phone." He felt a small but temporary twinge of guilt that he had not tried to call Blair's cell phone, it just hadn't occurred to him. He would call her after he talked to Humboldt.

"You sound worried, sir. What do you think has happened?"

"I just don't know. We've had some threats, you know. And some of them were against Blair. I wasn't here today, but there's a sign of some damage to the wall in the kitchen. I hate to speculate, but I want to find her."

"We could send a patrol car to pick you up, sir. And we could put out a BOLO on the car, if you want."

"Yes, yes, that's a good idea. And I'll look for you soon here. You have my address?"

"Yes, sir. We'll get there as soon as we can."

"Thank you, Matt. I appreciate it."

***

Melanie had taken off the chic outfit she'd worn for the trip to the election center and managed to hang it up instead of throwing it on other clothes in a pile on a chair in her bedroom. This morning she had put on comfy sweat pants and a torn, extra large Emory t-shirt.

　　　　　　　LEILA RYLAND SWAIN

Enough professionalism for one day. She poured a glass of mint iced tea and lounged on her sofa to check emails. She was ignoring the camera and procrastinated taking out the memory card and putting it in the computer to upload yesterday's photos. The shoot at the election center had been a big disappointment, really, because she didn't get the picture she wanted of Viktor messing with the machines. A doll! That's what he'd pulled from his pocket and then dangled in front of her.

So she'd failed in her assignment, and she hated having to tell the others that she'd failed. Walter Dobbs, especially. He'd become a hero to her just in that one afternoon she spent with him here, with Blair and Henry, and then Hallie. She'd later studied his resume on Wikipedia and knew she'd been privileged to meet a person of his substance and character. She had wanted desperately to please him, see a shine in his eyes when he looked at her. Now he would dismiss her as inconsequential and ineffective. That hurt. Her heart felt weighted and sore.

That evening, her cell phone rang. She saw it was Dick calling and punched talk, wondering what he wanted with her now. His voice was loud and aggrieved in her ear as he ranted about Blair not being at home when he arrived, nor was the Porsche, and that he had no transportation.

"No, Blair's not here, and I haven't seen her or talked to her." She knew he didn't believe her. And where was Blair? What had happened? She dialed Blair's cell, and got a recording. "Blair? Where are you, honey? I've just had a mad call from Dick. Call me, please." There was nothing she could do about it at the moment but a knot of anxiety began in her stomach.

She finally inserted the memory card into the slot on the computer and loaded the pictures from the day. There was Viktor holding that stupid doll in front of him, flapping it in her face like some overgrown child. The picture was blurred by the movement of the doll, but she had seen it: one of those Russian stacking dolls that apparently had some meaning, but she had no idea what that was. As she looked more closely at the pictures, in the next one she saw something behind his back, a faint image, a partial image almost out of view. She cropped the picture so the image was large and in the center of the picture. And damned if it wasn't a thumb drive being stuck into a machine slot. By golly, she had her picture, her evidence, her credibility and acceptance. She had to tell Henry—and Walter—and Blair, if she could find her.

CHAPTER TWENTY-SIX

Blair sat on the comfortable sofa in the Perry's living room, her legs stretched out on an ottoman Henry's mother had pushed toward her. "Please, Mrs. Miller, just rest now." Margaret Perry sat nearby and took up knitting from a basket beside her chair. The click of the needles and Margaret's soft voice had a calming effect on Blair's reeling thoughts. She had been sitting here in Henry's home for thirty minutes now, numb and frightened. She had wanted to see Melanie, but Hallie had convinced her it wouldn't be safe to be there now, and she had to agree. She shuffled in the chair, loosening her limbs, and looked around. An old clock on the mantel over a fireplace caught her notice—it was beautiful and reminded her of the clocks her grandfather had collected and repaired. She had loved being with him among the chiming of the various clocks and learning to tell time. He would set the hands and say *now what time is this?* Her mother had sold most of the clocks to finance the debut and the wedding. The clock on the mantel chimed out five gongs, and Margaret smiled. "My husband will be home any time now, and I know he'll be glad to meet you."

Blair cleared her throat and tried to speak. Her voice came out wobbly at first; she wasn't sure she could form words yet. "I'm….so grateful for your taking me in, Mrs. Perry." She paused for a long moment, looking at the woman who had welcomed her. "I had….no place else….to go. At the moment."

"We understand. Henry's put your car in a friend's garage to keep it safe until you need it. The keys are right here on the mantel."

"I just have to figure things out a bit—I don't know what to do next quite yet."

"You're welcome here as long as you need to be."

Something began to smell delicious from further back in the house, and Margaret put her knitting away and rose. "I have to check on dinner. May I get you something to drink—iced tea, coffee, water, maybe?"

"I'd love some coffee, actually, I'll come with you."

She followed Margaret through the dining room and into the kitchen, which had windows looking out over the spacious backyard. The sun was sinking down behind the houses next to the back fence and a spreading shade was settling over the yard. Margaret poured coffee for her and offered half and half, which she declined, accepting a couple of teaspoons of sugar. Blair stood at the window and studied the backyard. Henry was there, sitting in a chair by a fire pit circled by rocks, looking at his phone.

"I'd like to go out back, if that's okay," she said, patting her pockets to locate her cell phone. "I'll just get my phone from my backpack."

"Fine. Dinner's on when my husband gets home."

"Thank you. It smells delicious."

Blair took her backpack out to the backyard and turned on her cell phone. As she expected, there were several calls from Dick, each one more threatening than the last. A call from Melanie, which she decided not to return just at the moment. She needed to try to understand what was going on in her inner world. She had run away from home. She had run away from her marriage, which had become more and more abusive. She had to confront the denial that had kept her in the marriage and confront the reality of her situation now that she'd left. Dick was not going to let her go easily. And where would she go, what would she do?

When she approached him, Henry got up and took her over to the dog pen. The dog she'd brought was happily playing with another dog, a beagle, whom Henry said was his dog, named Fetch. Blair's dog was not of a determinate breed but was larger than Fetch and had a red coat with a white vest and nose stripe. "Well, I'll name my dog Carry, then. Like that old song…comin' for to carry me home. Here, Carry!" she called. The dog came right over, wagging his tail.

An old black Ford pulled into the driveway and parked in front of the garage. "There's Dad." Henry accompanied his father toward where Blair was standing, and introduced them. "Blair, my father,

                    LEILA RYLAND SWAIN

Beko Perry. Blair Miller's visiting us for a little while." Beko extended his hand and she took it and found a warm clasp and a pleasant vibe. His face crinkled in a smile. "You are most welcome here, Mrs. Miller. I'm going to wash up before dinner. Your mother is making dinner, Henry?'

"Of course, yes, let's go in."

"Where is your brother?"

"He was skateboarding just up the street. I'll go call him."

Beko said to Blair, "Let's see what the mother is making. I expect it will be good." Blair smiled and followed him in the back door.

She had just sat down at the dining table with Margaret and Beko when Henry reappeared with Jordan in tow, crowing about how he'd beat his friend Freddy on two out of three jumps. He saw Blair and stopped in mid-sentence.

"This is my son Jordan, Mrs. Miller," Beko said. "He forgets his manners sometimes. Sit here, son."

"Hello." Jordan lowered his eyes, but Blair felt the heat of his gaze and the subdued anger and curiosity he emitted. The waves of his intensity struck her like a mallet in her chest.

She ate as much as she was able of the delicious chicken and rice, not wanting any of it but loathe to appear picky or rejecting of their food. She was surprised to realize she had felt comfortable there until Jordan joined the family. The atmosphere was homey, safe, and warm. Jordan made a crack in the space that she didn't understand, and she became conscious again of her bruised face that no one else had seemed to notice. Jordan noticed. He glanced at her quickly and his eyes met hers. The flicker in his eyes was unreadable. She shivered.

She was to spend the night there, although she thought perhaps she should go to a hotel. But Henry persuaded her she would be safer there and told her that the State Police had put out a BOLO on the Porsche. He was going to bunk with Jordan, and his room was hers for the night. They would decide what to do tomorrow. She slid between clean sheets and sank immediately into a dreamless sleep.

***

Dick loved riding in the state police car. He sat up front beside the driver, who in his pressed dark blue uniform and badges on the front exuded an air of authority. Who had a gun in the holster along his leg and probably another one strapped to his chest inside his shirt. Who was totally in his service. One of the most fun things of Dick's office had turned out to be having the police working for him instead of against him. This is what power was and he was going to use it to find his wife and his Porsche. She was not going to spoil his election chances.

Officer Stocks had picked him up at his house at seven and the light was fading. The police car ride improved his mood. He knew Stocks from previous rides, and was glad to be with him. That Officer Stocks was Black didn't seem to register with Dick. He was police, which set him apart.

"Where do you want to go, Sir?" Officer Stocks spoke in a monotone, never taking his eyes off the highway. They were now proceeding south on I-75 toward downtown Atlanta.

"Melanie's." Dick was looking out the window at Atlanta skyline and had fallen into a depressive state of mind. He was certain he'd find Blair at Melanie's apartment, and then what? Would she come back with him to their home? What kind of argument, force, would he be required to use? In front of the police? No, he had to put these thoughts aside. He'd figure out what to do when he saw Blair, maybe she would fall into his arms and weep. She was waiting for him to rescue her. Maybe he'd forgive her.

"Sir, do you have an address?" The officer now glanced briefly at Dick, who had huddled against the door.

"Address? Just drive down to Sweet Auburn and I'll show you the house." Dick had no idea what the address was, but he knew where Melanie lived, of course he did, he'd been there before. Or had he?

The officer left I-75 at exit #285C, Freedom Parkway, and pulled over to the right lane to turn on Boulevard. He made a couple more turns, waiting for Dick to tell him where to go. Suddenly Dick lurched forward in his seat, waving his arm. "There it is—there's the church— that church where Tammy sings. I was there once, and heard her sing.

　　　　　　　　　　　　　　LEILA RYLAND SWAIN

Melanie's place is…on this street somewhere."

"What's Melanie's last name, Sir?"

Dick searched his inventory of names and came up short. "She's a photographer—*Atlanta Magazine*—all that crap—do you know her?"

The officer laughed, a deep chuckle. His wife was a big fan of her work. "Melanie Rutledge, Sir?"

Dick looked sharply at the officer. "That's her."

The officer called into his station and quickly had Melanie's address.

Dick stood on the sidewalk looking at the house number the officer had given him and realized he'd never been there before. Steps led up to the front door on a porch, and there were also steps on the side of the house going down to a basement. He took a gamble and went up the steps and knocked on the front door. A middle aged Black woman came to the door. "Can I help you?" She did not open the screen door and stood partially in shadow.

"I'm looking for Melanie—the photographer—Melanie?"

Dick felt oddly off balance under the gaze of this composed woman, as if his fly was unzipped or he was in some way not fully dressed.

"Melanie Rutledge lives downstairs." Her tone offered no further information or help, so Dick said "thanks" and trudged back down the stone steps, and the other steps to the basement. He had to duck his head to get under the ledge of the porch to get to the door.

It seemed like five minutes before Melanie opened the door. "Dick, Blair is not here. I haven't seen or heard from her today, I told you that on the phone."

"I don't believe you." Dick pushed through the door and Melanie stepped aside to avoid being knocked down.

"How dare you, Dick. I didn't say you could come in, this is an intrusion."

"I know you're hiding her here." He walked through the apartment, flung open the bathroom door, went in the kitchen and wrenched the pantry door open. "Where are you, Blair? Come on out, Daddy's here now." He opened the back door, walked out on a small ground-level porch and looked around the small fenced-in yard. He walked around the yard and peered behind several large bushes. He looked over the low fence into an alley and saw only garbage cans.

Walking back to the living room, he pounded the top of the dining table with his fist. "I know she was here. You alerted her to run out the back and through the alley. I'll find her."

Melanie just stared at him and snorted. "Please get out of my apartment, Dick."

"You know, Melanie, you've never been anything but a bad influence on Blair. You know where she is, and when I find her, you both will pay, big time. I guarantee that."

"Officer, this man is an intruder in my apartment. I demand that he leave now, or I will call your superiors."

The officer moved to take Dick's arm but he wrestled it away and stalked out the front door. He yelled over his shoulder through clenched teeth, "You're going to hear from me, Melanie." The officer followed him up the steps and out to the street.

In the car, Officer Stocks moved out of the parking space and down the street. There was no traffic to speak of at this hour and the streets seemed eerily quiet except for a radio spilling out rock music somewhere in one of the houses.

"Just cruise around this neighborhood a bit, Stocks. We might see my wife on the street after she left Melanie's."

Stocks obliged Dick for a half hour or so, circling a few blocks around Melanie's apartment and looking down alleys. The police radio chattered away with reports of breaking and entering and lookouts and other often indecipherable communications, in a broken on and off fashion. "Damn, Stocks, that radio is irritating." Dick was growing more and more frustrated that he didn't see Blair anywhere and didn't know what else to do. He was getting hungry. "Anyplace around here to get some fast eats, Stocks?"

"Yes, sir, I could use some food too. There's a J. R. Crickets just around the corner. Best wings and shrimp in town."

"Never been there. Will I see anybody I know?"

Officer Stocks laughed. "I doubt it. But we can get some take-out. Trust me."

The patrol car pulled into the lot and parked in front of the

                    LEILA RYLAND SWAIN

restaurant. Groups of people were hanging around the tables out front, laughing and generally having a good time. A man with a ragged white beard approached the passenger side of the car with his hand held out.

"Hungry, sir, just need a buck, sir, to get a few wings."

Stocks shooed the man away while Dick shrank back in his seat. "I'll bring you a selection, Secretary. Just keep your window rolled up. No harm here. I'll be right back."

Dick locked the car. He pulled out his phone to check and see if he had a message from Blair. No one was calling him. His fury and frustration grew and he kicked the dashboard repeatedly until his foot was tired. Stocks returned with plates of wings and fries and he gobbled the food down, sucking the meat off the sweet bones and cramming fries in his mouth. He handed his empty container to Stocks like a child handing his left-over trash to his mother.

When Stocks returned from the trash can, his radio was squawking. Both he and Dick were pulled to the crackling announcement that there was a BOLO hit on a red Porsche, license plate RCF8832 on Auburn Avenue, N. E. A suspect was in custody. The squawking became too mangled to understand the words. Dick pumped his fist in the air and shouted., "It's Blair! They've got her. Let's go, Stocks."

CHAPTER TWENTY-SEVEN

Jordan could hardly believe his mother and father had taken in the wife of the odious Secretary of State, who Jordan knew was behind the efforts to suppress the votes in the next election. He dared not speak up about this at the dinner table. His father had reprimanded him about his manners and that was a warning. The family was being hospitable to her, she had the purple bruising around her eye, so maybe there were things he didn't know about. But he didn't have to like her even if he had to keep his mouth shut. She had smiled at him, but that meant nothing. She was just a rich white woman and he had little use for those types. Had that air of white superiority that no smile could banish.

The dog that came with her was okay, though. Jordan went out to the back yard with her and Henry after dinner and petted the dog, named Carry. He licked his hand and wagged his tail when Jordan scratched his ears. The dog could stay. Blair asked Henry about where the Porsche was, which Jordan guessed was her husband's car. Henry told her it was in his friend Darrien's garage and was safe until she needed it. Henry asked her if she wanted to call her husband and tell him where she was. She said "No!" She sounded scared and that softened Jordan a bit, but not much.

The mention of the Porsche galvanized Jordan's interest and attention. He would give anything to see the Porsche, just see it and run his hands over the curves, caress the flow and the polish of the finest car in the world. He'd seen a picture in one of his car magazines, and the longing to see one for real felt like a wound in his heart. He didn't speak of his feelings, just stuck his hands in his pockets and scuffed the dirt to cover their intensity from the woman. You just didn't let a white person see what you wanted. It's a lesson he'd learned early on. She was

     LEILA RYLAND SWAIN

not his friend, even if everybody else in the family was acting all post-racial togetherness. He made a face that she wouldn't see, petted Carry another couple of times, and went in the house.

Who can say whether Henry knew Jordan overheard him tell Blair the keys to the Porsche were on the mantel in the living room. That's where Jordan couldn't resist going, picking up a candle for cover as he palmed the key, the next best thing to running a hand over the fender. Just to jingle it and dream about what it would feel like if that key was to his Porsche and then to slip it in his pocket, to just for a moment think the car was his, that he could drive it around and everyone would gawk at him.

His mother called him and asked him to take out the trash and in his haste to do that job, the key did not get put back on the mantel. Outside, the night was brisk but beautiful and after dumping the trash, he wandered around to Freddy's house two streets over. His friend happened to be the brother of Darrien, who was sheltering the car. Jordan didn't have a conscious intention, really, to place himself in the vicinity of the car. He often shot baskets at Freddie's driveway hoop and that was what he thought they would do, if he thought at all.

What happened next is still under dispute in the family. Why did Jordan get arrested while behind the wheel of the Porsche two blocks down from Freddy and Darrien's house? The story Jordan told is that Darrien said he could just "drive it around the block" and come right back. The story Dick Miller, Secretary of the State of Georgia, told is that Jordan Perry was stealing his car.

***

Henry sat up in the living room reading a book on constitutional law, after his parents and Blair had gone to bed. When the grandfather clock struck ten, he looked up and simultaneously realized Jordan had not come home and that the key to the Porsche was not on the mantel. His mind froze. *What the hell? Did Jordan take the key? Or maybe Blair took it to my room with her?* He sat for a few minutes sorting out his thoughts. He didn't want to bother Blair because she might be asleep already and if Jordan did lift it, Henry wanted to track it down before reporting anything to her. His mind was spinning and he felt dizzy and afraid.

Henry left the house quietly and headed toward Darrien's house, cutting through an open back yard to get to the next street over. As soon as he left that yard to get out on the street, he saw two police cruisers, roof lights rotating and flashing, just a block down. He broke into a run and was panting by the time he saw, first, the Porsche parked by the curb, and second, his brother on the ground beside a police cruiser. When he saw Dick Miller standing with a uniformed policeman, he skidded to a stop. His friend Darrien was pleading with the officer and Henry could hear his shouts. His assessment of the situation was swift: Jordan had taken the key and had persuaded Darrien to let him drive the car around the block. There was a BOLO on the car and a roaming cruiser spotted it, Jordan at the wheel. Henry's heart thumped madly and thoughts spun wildly in his head. What was he to do?

He took some deep breaths and walked toward the scene. Jordan was face down on the asphalt, his head turned to the side. His nose was bloody and his eyes were closed.

Henry dropped to his knees beside his brother, shivering violently and shouted, "Jordan! What happened?"

The police officer yanked him up by the arms and said, "Get away. He's under arrest." He pushed Henry hard and Henry stumbled, catching his balance with effort. When he looked up, he was facing the Secretary of State, Dick Miller.

"Henry, what are you doing here? Do you know this person who was stealing my car?"

"That's my brother, Jordan. He was not stealing your car, I'm sure of that. He's just a kid.

Have you called an ambulance for him?" Henry's voice was agitated, his speech frenzied. "Let me see how he is. Have you killed him?"

"He's fine. My car disappeared from my house today and the police were searching for it. They called me a half hour ago, said they spotted the car being driven by that boy, who you say is your brother. He was

                    LEILA RYLAND SWAIN

stealing it, and he's going to jail. We're taking him there now. So just get out of the way."

The officer had lifted Jordan off the ground and he groaned weakly as he was dragged to the police car and stuffed in the back seat, where he slumped over. Henry turned to the car, but Miller caught his arm. "He's going to jail now."

Henry shook off his hand and twisted away. "Take your hands off me, Mr. Miller. We'll see you in court."

"Now, Henry, don't get aggressive with me. We are also searching for my wife, who took the car from our home today. Please tell me if you have any information about her whereabouts."

Henry did not respond. His jaw was clamped shut, and he stood, mute, staring at his former employer.

"Well, we'll get that information out of your brother. Surely he knows where she is." Miller turned away, dangling the key to the Porsche. "Okay, then, we're off. Officer, I'll follow you to the precinct so I can file the charges. Goodbye, Henry." Miller folded himself into the Porsche and pulled out behind the car holding Jordan. He did not look back at Henry as he drove away.

Henry wiped his eyes and mopped his head with a handkerchief, willing his anger to lessen so he could think. When he looked around again, he realized that his friend Darrien and his younger brother were standing nearby all the while.

"What the hell, Darrien, how did Jordan get access to the car? I trusted you to take care of it." Darrien's brother was crying and rubbing his eyes with his fists.

"Damn it, Henry, this here nub of a brother let him have a spin around the block. I didn't know about it until I saw the car leave the garage and I couldn't stop it. I ran after him, then the police caught him. There was a BOLO out on it." He punched his brother on the shoulder and the boy wept harder.

"I left the key on the mantel and Jordan saw it and took it. We'd been talking about the car and where it was and I guess the temptation to see it was just too much. And then he went too far. And you let him."

"I'm sorry, Henry. And you worthless boy, you sorry too, right?" Freddy mumbled an apology through his tears.

"For God's sake, don't talk to the police about this if they come back to question you, and they probably will. Just say you need a lawyer. I'm going home to see what we can do about this damage."

"Okay, Henry, I understand. And whatever we can do…" Darrien sighed and pulled his brother after him toward their home.

Henry jogged back to his house to break the news, a heaviness in his heart he'd never known before. This was his fault, and everyone would suffer for his mistakes. He'd implicated his parents and his brother in the effort to protect Blair, and he should not have done that. What would happen to all of them because of him, and how must he act to salvage the situation? It seemed a moment for him to stand up and exercise his better judgment and whatever legal skills he had acquired. It was up to him. He feared he would fail.

CHAPTER TWENTY-EIGHT

Friday, July 27

Viktor's mother had not visited him in Atlanta for several years. She didn't like the traffic around the city and would only come if her daughter would drive. Lara was usually busy with two small boys and her husband, so it took something urgent to get Viktor's sister marshaled for a trip. Viktor received a phone call from his mother at seven o'clock in the evening after he had returned from the trip to the election center at Kennesaw State. Some synchronicity between mother and son was at work, for obsessive thoughts had begun in the afternoon and he brooded on a desperate neediness for maternal attention. He had crashed in his lounge chair, exhausted, and when the phone rang, he knew before he answered it was his mother calling.

"Viktor, son, your sister and I are driving to Atlanta tomorrow to see you." She spoke in her native tongue to him and the Russian language was music to his ears just then. She had learned English but had always spoken in Russian to her children and to her husband. Viktor was fairly fluent in the language, but rarely had a chance to speak it except to his students and a few colleagues, and to her.

"I will be happy to see you both," he responded in kind. Viktor meant these words as never before. The doll his mother gave him had taken him just so far, but her magic was dwindling. He understood the doll ceased communication the moment he put the thumb drive in the election machine slot at Kennesaw State. He took that as an ominous sign, but he couldn't interpret it. His mother, Olga Smirnov Durov, would tell him what it meant.

"I have urgent news for you, son, but I don't want to say it over the telephone."

"Yes, yes, I will wait patiently here for you." Viktor knew her news would be her insight into why the doll had failed him. He could not relax. He circled his apartment many times, counting steps, breathing, and trying to ease the tension in his mind. After tossing and turning in his bed for an hour, he put on his coat and left the apartment. The night had turned cooler and a wind swept down the lane in front of his building. Dark clouds scuttled across the sky. He hunched in his coat and let the darkness surround him. He found comfort in the loneliness of the gray buildings with a few lit windows. A few other sleepless wraiths drifted on the winding paths around the garden and the fenced-off utilities areas. Viktor's mood was bleak. Hallie was lost to him. Even if he could reestablish a relationship with her, he worried that his mother would object to it. He had committed an act at the Election Center that would never be understood. As he stood at the dark pool at the center of the garden, an urge to throw himself in the water and drown came over him. He thrust off his coat and stooped to untie his shoes, and when he did this he felt the doll shift in his pocket. That damned doll! He reached in his pocket, pulled out the doll, and threw it in the lake. It bobbed up and down a couple of times, like a cork on a fish line, and then sank through the dark waters until it was out of sight.

He clapped his hand on his head. *My god, why did I do that?* But when that thought settled, a peaceful feeling crept into his disordered brain. The doll was gone, and that felt right. Unless he wanted to jump in and dig around in the muck to find it again. He laughed out loud. *Good riddance.* Viktor grabbed his coat and wrapped it around him tightly, lifted his head to the stars sailing out from behind the drifting clouds, and walked home.

Viktor escorted his mother and sister around Atlanta to the sights they had enjoyed on previous visits. The Botanical Garden was high on the list. Olga took his arm as they paused at the mosaiculture Earth Goddess, while Lara wandered off taking photographs with her phone. Mother and son strolled down to the Glade, where the reflection of the saffron Chihuly tower shone in the rectangular pool. Viktor's vivid remembrance of his encounter there with Anatoly Oblomov, and the request he made, gripped his mind. Although it was a cool day, sweat trickled down his back. He shivered.

                    LEILA RYLAND SWAIN

"Let's sit here on this bench, son," Olga said, patting the space beside her as she took her seat. "I told you I had urgent news, but I didn't want to talk about it while Lara was around; she has heard this earlier."

Viktor sat beside her and found a pleasurable safety in her close presence, just as he always had as a child.

"Your brother, Alexander Dimitri Durov is dead."

"Oh my God." He put his head in his hands and groaned as if a knife had been stuck in his ribs.

"Please don't take the Lord's name in vain, Viktor. He died of a heart attack in Paris four days ago. His wife sent me a telegram." Olga's hands were folded in her lap and she stared steadily at the saffron column. "I know you did not know him, but he was my first born and always in my heart. He fought for the truth and ideals that impassioned him, and for that I respect him. He felt it was his duty to resist the evils of the Russian state." She looked at Viktor. "You, my second son, must take up the challenges that face us here in this, our adopted country." She reached for his hand and squeezed it. "Yes, that is what our nature calls us to—we must not be complacent in the face of evil. Your father was disappointed that Alexander did not come to America and that he chose rebellion. Although I was heartbroken not to have him by my side, I felt a deep satisfaction in his calling." She sighed and released his hand.

Viktor felt numb and stared at his mother. "Are you certain...it was a...natural death?"

"Quite certain. He had left Russia and was in hiding with his wife. His heart was never strong, and he died in his sleep. An autopsy revealed the cause. Yes, his adversaries were searching for him, but they did not find him."

Lara was walking slowly down the path to the Glade pointing her phone at the tower and the water mirror. Viktor spoke quickly before she reached them. "Mother, you cannot know what effect this news has on me. There are circumstances I cannot speak of at the moment, and I need time to absorb this news and see what it means to me in certain situations." He saw the alarm on her face and his words tumbled out.

"No, no, nothing to be alarmed about. Just a personal matter. I will tell you all about it very soon."

He rose to greet Lara and to let his emotions disperse. He could put his feelings into separate compartments for a time, and would pull them out later to grapple with. He stood with his sister to admire the saffron tower and agreed with her, in English, that Chihuly was indeed a very fine artist.

CHAPTER TWENTY-NINE

Hallie shook her head like a retriever after a swim in the ocean, and droplets from her freshly washed hair sprayed around the sink and floor. The tune from a remembered old song made her smile: *I'm gonna wash that man right out of my hair.* It used to come on the radio when she was small and her mother liked it. Her mother thought the show in which the song was sung, *South Pacific*, was against racism, and she would sing another of the songs: *You've got to be carefully taught…to hate and fear…to be afraid of people whose skin is a different shade….* Hallie had regarded her mother as the oracle and still thought of her every day. She was the reason Hallie went to college and to grad school to get a master's in psychology. Hallie wanted to understand the psychology of racism and had pursued that goal with passion.

When she read *Beloved*, Toni Morrison's classic novel, she wept. The main character, Sethe, slashed her daughter's throat with a chainsaw to keep her from being enslaved, and Hallie knew her mother would have killed her too to keep her from being a slave. What was this Thing that made people hate? Her study of Carl Jung carried her deep into the human psyche and what he called "the shadow." She had concluded, along with other scholars, that white people hated their shadow, projected it onto those with black skin, and tried to control them. If they couldn't, they killed them. That was the essence. Oh, she could elaborate on the topic with countless examples and branching arguments, which she often did to her classes, but it all came back to the same conclusion.

As she dried her hair with a soft towel and soaked up the moisture, she considered the problem of Viktor. And considered what Walter Dobbs had led her to understand so clearly that afternoon in her basement. If Viktor was in love with her with a sincere heart, then she, Hallie, had a power she could exercise, if she chose to do so. But was he in love with her? He had not declared himself, although certainly his actions constituted courtship. Attended church with her, nice dinners at good restaurants, and his interest in her was obvious. But was it a devious interest? And, more importantly perhaps, was she in love with him?

Viktor had told her he was working with Secretary of State Miller, and as she recalled it now, he said "to help manage the vote." At the time, she didn't pay enough attention to that. What did he mean? He had also talked about visiting the lynching museum and seemed to be moved by it. He had essentially asked her to trust him on this and she had allowed herself to do so—to a certain extent. His attention was wonderful and she had basked in it like a flower coming to bloom and had redone her hair, thinking to please him. Now, she thought she must have been crazy to collapse into his arms like that.

Collapse into his arms? No, she had not literally done that and she regretted that figure of speech. Her hand on his arm. A chaste kiss. That was all. But she chided herself for what her imagination had done with that. Yes, her attraction to him, her fantasies. She acknowledged all of that, ruefully. *Why am I attracted to a white man, a foreigner of Russian birth?* She didn't have a good answer to that question. And why would Viktor take up with a Black woman? That was another question she had no answer to.

Hallie had never worn the dress she bought in Ethiopia last summer. She knew it was a weird aspect of her psyche to buy nice things—luxurious nightgowns, expensive soaps, tissue-silk scarves— and put them away and wait maybe years to use them. Somehow it felt comforting to know these treasures were there even as she would wear the washed-thin flannel pajamas and bathe with a plain cake of Ivory soap. But today she would wear the black off-the-shoulder dress, rich nubby layers of black and cream cotton fringed at the elbow-length sleeves and hem. The African women who designed and constructed these dresses were the finest of artists, working with local weavers and making their own dyes from natural plants.

As she smoothed it over her hips, she looked again into the eyes of

     LEILA RYLAND SWAIN

the robed woman with wide bands of etched silver on her arms and a swinging pendant on her bony chest. Hallie asked her about the black ornament on the chain, an open palm, fingers pointing downward, studded with green gems. The woman told her the amulet was a hamsa and was protection against the evil eye. When Hallie opened the package containing her dress at the hotel, she found a small hamsa on a silver chain tucked into the folds. Now, she rummaged in her jewelry box and found the necklace and slipped it around her neck. Perhaps it would provide the protection against the evil eye she might encounter in her meeting with Viktor this afternoon. When she looked in the mirror, she almost didn't recognize her own self—her natural hair, the elegant African dress—and she took a bow.

***

Hallie gave Viktor an address: 100 Ivan Allen, Jr. Boulevard. She said it was near the Aquarium. He was to meet her there. He called an Uber at 2: 30 p.m. and was startled when it pulled up at an unusual building downtown, one he had often noticed. Stark in design, the architecture reminded Viktor of a stockade—a giant slab the color of clay guarded the building. He had not been there before, nor had he known what the building housed. When he exited the cab, he saw the lettering on the driveway wall: Center for Civil and Human Rights Museum. Of course. He had read that the structure was designed by an architect involved with the African Heritage Museum in D.C. Some understanding of what was perhaps to come jolted him. He caught his breath.

He saw her sitting on a bench near the entrance. She had not seen him yet and was straight of back and poised, her head turned away from him. He saw her profile in silhouette and a ray of light bounced around her hair and it glimmered as if ablaze. She turned and saw him. She rose with grace and raised her hand in greeting, but did not move toward him. Viktor hurried to her side. She looked ravishing— her hair? A lovely dress?

She had bought tickets. She smiled at him and headed toward

the door, which he pulled open for her, then she moved slowly into the foyer. Viktor followed, looking around. An entire wall displayed a giant fist raised over the assembly of wandering people, shooting rays of energy and color and words. Justice! That word shouted into the air without making a sound. He was propelled back into the aura of the lynching museum, and the same shiver that he had then ran down his spine. He tried to take Hallie's hand but she twisted away with a smile cast over her shoulder. She beckoned him on.

They entered a hall with honey-colored wall panels inscribed with quotations from Martin Luther King, Jr. Cases displayed his papers and some personal items. He saw a worn suitcase with toiletries beside it and wanted to linger to examine it, but Hallie pulled him onward. Some urgency paled her face and tightened her shoulders, and the grasp of her hand was a claw. "Come on, you can come back and look at that later if you want to," she said.

They passed a less interesting exhibit on global human rights and arrived at a spacious gallery introduced by words painted on glass over the entrance: ROLL DOWN LIKE WATER. "This," Hallie said, "is the place." They slid into seats side by side at a lunch counter modeled on the 1960 Woolworth's in Greensboro, North Carolina. They stared at a photograph blown-up and stretched across the wall behind the counter depicting the crowd of people (white) harassing those who sat in demanding service for Blacks. Headphones lay on the counter, and Hallie tenderly placed them on his ears. He turned up the volume and the sound of the mob behind the students at the counter blasted his brain. He closed his eyes and endured. "Nigger, go back where you came from." "You not allowed to eat here." "We gon lynch yore body in the nearest tree." And on and on, the students had sat, assaulted, trained not to move or react.

When he looked up, Hallie was gone, and he was alone to wipe the tears from his eyes. He managed to walk toward the next gallery in the exhibit but doubted whether he would manage what more would be thrown at him. The large, white space he entered was a relief. The video playing on a curved wall depicted a crowd surging around the Lincoln Memorial in Washington and beside the Reflecting Pool. He

          LEILA RYLAND SWAIN

found Hallie there, standing like a soldier, and together they listened to the sound of Martin Luther King's voice, *"…the Negro lives on a lonely island of poverty in the midst of a vast ocean of material prosperity…Now is the time to make justice a reality for all of God's children…"* The man's face shone on the screen in the midst of the crowds around him and his deep mellow voice filled the room. Viktor was in awe. *"I have a dream today…I have a dream that one day every valley shall be exalted… every hill and mountain shall be made low. The rough places will be made plain, and the crooked places will be made straight. And the glory of the Lord shall be revealed, and all flesh shall see it together. This is our hope."*

Music poured from the speakers, gospel songs, people chanting, black and white together. Viktor felt something move in his soul and he was touched with a new feeling, almost a spiritual thing. He tried to take Hallie's hand but she turned from him. They walked on to the next gallery in silence. Viktor's mind was numb and racing at the same time, he was deeply impressed and struggled with shame. Shame, even though he had not even been alive when those events happened, but shame because he had not fully understood what was at stake here. He wiped sweat from his face with a handkerchief. .

Darkness assaulted him as he entered the next gallery. Viktor's eyes shifted to adjust to the abrupt change, the absence of light, the absence of sensory clues. Then the blare of the radio, *"King shot in Memphis!"* A cacophony of agitated news anchors reporting the story, funky rhythm and blues music that he hated, politicians exhorting the nation to remain calm. Waves of hysterical sound washed over him and he stuck his fingers in his ears. Hallie was staring at him but he couldn't read the expression on her face. Was it a frown? What was she conveying of her feelings? What did she want from him? She beckoned and led him to stairs going up to a landing over the scene. Photos of bloodstains, neon-it sign Lorraine Motel. He got it: this is where Dr. King was shot, here on this balcony.

He was dizzy and needed to get out of here. "I'll meet you out front in a few minutes." He touched Hallie's shoulder and headed back down the stairs. He doubled back through the galleries to the front door and sat on a bench in a grassy area on the left side of the building.

He would see Hallie when she came out and he hoped he would be ready to have a conversation with her. He was not sure he would. Sweat dripped from his brow onto the collar of his shirt. His head hurt, his mind full of agitated thoughts, and his heart thumped in his chest. He shut his eyes and felt he was in a cocoon, swaddled in cotton batting, and some kind of beat, a rhythm, flowed through his body and he was still for a while.

When he opened his eyes, the sun had sunk lower in the sky and he sensed he'd been out for some time. His watch said 4:30, he'd entered the building at 3. He didn't see Hallie. He stood up, feeling shaky but walked steadily to the front door of the building. The guard at the door told him the museum was closing at 5, but that he could walk through to look for his friend. He went through all the galleries once more and she was not there.

CHAPTER THIRTY

Lights burned in the Perry house until dawn Thursday night. Curious but respectful neighbors pushed aside curtains to watch. A Lincoln town car arrived at midnight, and a driver opened the door for a large older man, who disappeared into the house and did not leave. The driver could be seen sitting in the kitchen drinking a cup of coffee. As the sun rose, the man came out of the house with Henry and the car pulled away from the curb and moved down the street.

A few minutes later, a young woman parked her car in front of the Perry house, went in and came out arm in arm with another young woman leading a red dog on a leash. After that, the neighbors saw nothing more out of the ordinary and the street settled into a late July sunshine. Leaves drifted down from trees onto growing piles swirled by the wind and scattered far from home.

Jordan dozed in the same cell in which he'd been thrown after his arrest earlier in the year. The man with the long nails that clacked on the stone floor was gone. He was alone. A medic had patched the wound on his head and determined that he was not seriously injured. He was questioned by the officer in charge, who knew who he was from his previous arrest even though he had no identification in his pockets. Lack of a driver's license was another charge on his rap sheet. Jordan did not see any advantage in trying to hide how he had gotten the key to the Porsche or where the Secretary of State's wife was. His state of mind was lucid even though his head throbbed.

Don't feel guilty about telling the cops where the man's wife was. That, or get my head busted open and I wasn't 'bout to be some kinda martyr to a secret that was going to be found out anyway. They just had to ask Darrien and Freddie 'cause they knew where she was. And in fact, she caused the whole mess by bringing that car into the hood.

Jordan sat up on the side of the bunk and munched on the biscuits the officer had brought him earlier. A raw morning shined through the high window with bars in his cell. He wondered what would happen next and whether Uncle Walter would be called and if he'd come and what he'd tell him and if he'd understand.

Should've just looked at the car. Didn't need to drive it and get Darrien in trouble too. Dad's gonna be so mad. I don't want to face him. He don't understand how it is, like maybe he was never wanting something so bad that you just couldn't say no. I hope it's Uncle Walter who comes, not Dad.

Jordan's mind hurt from trying to sort it out. He lay back down on the bunk facing the wall. Sometime later, the officer unlocked the door to his cell and said, "You have a visitor."

The officer led him out to a room with a glass window and a telephone on the wall by the chair in front of the window. His brother Henry sat behind the glass.

✳✳✳

Monday, July 30

Henry shuddered as he drove up the winding driveway to the house of his former employer, Dick Miller. Uncle Walter's solid presence in the passenger seat was reassuring and helped him keep the anxiety at what awaited at bay. He parked the Camaro at the front steps and opened the door for the older man, who stepped out and stared in admiration at the imposing structure. "What a wonderful example of English Georgian architecture! I've admired and studied that style, but have not seen this one."

His uncle's interest in Dick Miller's house startled Henry and an awareness grew that perhaps he didn't know the man well at all. "Come on, let's not linger here in the driveway." Henry beckoned Uncle Walter to follow him up the steps to the front door.

Dick seemed to have been lurking behind the door as they

                    LEILA RYLAND SWAIN

climbed the stairs, because he flung it open just as they reached the landing. Henry was shocked at his appearance. Gray sweatpants hung precariously on his hips, and a faded t-shirt failed to cover his stomach, leaving his prominent belly button on display. His hair stuck out in untended spikes and his eyes were wild as he looked pointedly from one man to the other.

"Well, you've taken your own sweet time to get here." He stared at Walter. "Henry, where is the lawyer you said you were bringing with you today?"

"Let me introduce Walter Dobbs, esquire, distinguished Atlanta attorney, who happens to be my uncle."

"You don't say. Well, they come in all colors nowadays."

"It's a pleasure to meet you, Mr. Secretary." Walter smiled cordially, and offered his hand to Dick.

"Haven't I met you somewhere before?"

"I worked with the Urban League a number of years ago, and I believe our paths did cross once or twice."

Dick led them into the living room and on through to the kitchen, which was a mess. "Sorry for the condition here. See, I lost my wife and my housekeeper at the same time. I'm sure hoping I can get my wife back. I can always find another housekeeper."

He motioned them to chairs around the cluttered kitchen table. "Let's get down to business. You told me on the phone, Henry, that you wanted to talk to me about my wife—about Blair, and that means you know where she is. All you have to do is tell me where she is. Then we're finished here."

"We also need to talk about my brother, Jordan Perry, whom you have accused of stealing your car and who is locked up in jail and has been denied bail." Henry spoke in measured tones, clear but with undernotes of dark steel.

"That punk did steal my car, we caught him red-handed, and he'll be charged on Tuesday in court with felonious theft and driving without a license. Nothing to talk about here."

"Your wife has a different view of that, sir." Again, Henry's voice was calm with a knife's edge underneath, a blade that could cut deep.

"My wife! You dare to bring my wife into this." Dick jumped up and bounced around the kitchen like a bongo ball, ricocheting off cabinets and the stove. He stopped in front of Henry and wagged his finger in his face. "The question to be answered immediately is: where is Blair? Your punk brother said she was at your house, but when we got there she was gone. It seems now that you know where she is, and goddamit you're going to tell me now."

Dick grabbed Henry's arm, but Walter put a firm hand on his shoulder and pushed him back easily. "Mr. Secretary, we've come to discuss that and it would be helpful if you would sit down and listen." Walter's tone was mellow and pleasing and yet, implacable, hinting of icy depths.

Dick was thrown off his balance and grabbed a chair to steady himself. He shook his head and groaned deeply. He pulled out the chair and sat down.

Henry cleared his throat and began again, drawing on his best and most neutral voice to convey the information that Dick wanted, but could only have at a price. "Your wife, Blair, is in a safe place at the moment. She is recovering well from the beating she received here in this house, one that could well have caused her more injury than it did, but nevertheless is the cause for her determination to remain apart from you at the present time."

Dick stared at Henry. "Beating…beating….no, no, there was no beating, she would not listen to me, she insisted on…" Dick put his forehead on the kitchen table and his body sagged. Walter reached out again and touched him in support. Dick relaxed and sat up. The quiet in the room stretched out for a minute or two, and the quiet was steadying and seemed to compose the air around the kitchen into a hum like the work of bees in their hive.

"Look." Dick said. "I have been anxious…and upset…about the coming election. And I may not have been the best husband to Blair that I could, but I hope…I hope…she will forgive me." He scratched his head and looked at the two men sitting with him, at the impassive but not unkind looks on their faces. "So here you are, and you want something from me. What do you want?" He spread his hands out on

   LEILA RYLAND SWAIN

the table, large hands, and looked at them as if he had folded his cards.

Henry shifted in his chair, crossed his legs, and opened a file folder he'd placed on the kitchen table. "Here's the situation, Mr. Miller. Blair feels safe where she is at the moment, but she has agreed to talk to you under certain conditions."

"What the hell does she want in order to talk to me?" Dick rolled his eyes. "I'm her husband."

"She wants the charges against Jordan Perry to be dropped."

Dick hollered "No way!" and pushed at the table so that it almost tipped over. Walter caught it and righted it. "There's no way in hell I'm going to let that punk go scot free, even if he is your brother. He took my car. Period."

Henry had been counseled not to argue with Miller. He exchanged glances with Uncle Walter and closed his file folder. "It looks like we're done here." He and Walter pushed back their chairs and rose.

Dick charged up out of his chair, shaking his fist. "Yes, dammit, we're done. And you better believe I'm going to find that wife of mine if it's the last thing I do." He moved toward the back door and opened it, gesturing for the men to leave.

"I bid you a good evening, Mr. Secretary," Walter said. He and Henry walked from the kitchen into the living room and then out through the front door.

"Such an amazing structure," Walter said as they got in the car to leave.

CHAPTER THIRTY-ONE

Saturday, July 28

Blair woke to the smell of frying bacon wafting up from below. She turned over, let the dream drifting through her mind fade, and opened her eyes to bright sunlight shining through a lace-curtained window. A fan clicked on somewhere in the house and cool air blew out of vents on the floor.. For a moment, she didn't know where she was, but she was warm and safe and hungry.

She heard a voice downstairs and remembered that she was at Melanie's mother's house in Resaca. Melanie drove her here yesterday and turned around and drove right back to Atlanta so as not to raise any suspicions by her absence. Mrs. Rutledge had seemed a bit stressed about having Blair thrust on her, but was gracious in her polite Southern lady way. Blair observed her petting Carry, and giving him tidbits of something the dog liked very much, for he licked her hand and his tail was a rotor of wagging. So the deal was struck. Blair could stay with her for a while, and Doro (the name she wanted to be called) was happy to take care of the dog.

"We used to have a dog like this until my husband died, but I didn't think I could manage one by myself. Maybe I was wrong." Doro smiled fondly at Carry, and he sat at her feet with a gleam in his eye.

In the late afternoon they had dinner, a dish she said her maid had made for her, and there was enough to share. Blair and Doro sat opposite each other in the dining room off the kitchen. Blue woven place mats matched the cloth napkins and candles with some drippings were lighted with a bit of ceremony. Doro explained the tuna noodle casserole with crushed potato chips on top as one she had on Friday nights. "It's just a habit, one that marks the end of the weekdays. I am a creature of habit, so you may find me boring." She laughed delicately.

Despite remembering some of Melanie's complaints about her mother, Blair warmed to the woman and could see the solid, middle class comfort of her being and of the home. After dinner, Doro invited her into the den to watch TV. She liked the evening news, and although her channel was fixed to Fox news, she thought Blair would prefer CNN, so that's what they watched. Blair was not accustomed to the nightly news, but she was struck by Anderson Cooper's sophisticated presence and liked listening to him talk. The Boy Scouts had announced they would admit girls and Cooper had some guests to talk about that move.

"Were you a girl scout, Blair?" Doro seemed agitated by this news report. She had laid down her knitting to listen intently.

"Yes, I was. I liked most of it. I went to a camp in Cloudland named for the founder of the girl scouts, Juliette Low. That was fun, canoeing and swimming and learning to build fires."

Doro didn't answer her, but resumed knitting. She had said she was making a baby blanket for a friend's daughter.

"How about you, Doro? Were you a girl scout?"

Doro turned to look at her over the rim of her glasses and her eyes were angry. "I was a girl scout leader for a number of years when Melanie was growing up. The girls and the boys should be separate, as they have always been." She knitted another row. "I just cannot imagine how it would be for the girls to camp with the boys. Why, look at what's happening in the military since they admitted women."

"I haven't been keeping up with that. What's been happening?"

Doro sighed and put down her knitting. "Unspeakable things—the girls, the women are being abused terribly. And no one cares."

Abuse. That word rang in Blair's ears. Abuse. She had been abused by Dick Miller, who had vowed to love and honor her, who said he needed her, wanted her, couldn't live without her. How would she sort this out? At the moment, as the word rippled down into her soul, she didn't know. But today she was glad to be with this comfortable woman who was knitting and talking about it in a way that made her feel better.

Blair's cell phone rang. She excused herself and went out on the porch to answer when she saw Henry's name. The evening was cool and she shivered even though she enjoyed the freshness of the air.

"How's it going, Blair?" Henry's voice was tinged with anxiety and he seemed to be speaking from a deep pit.

"I'm okay. Mrs. Rutledge is kind." Blair sat down on the steps. "What's going on there?"

"I hate to have to tell you this, but Miller is adamant. Walter and I talked to him, but he said he'd never drop the charges against Jordan. Felony theft."

"So he doesn't want to talk to me?"

"I think he does, but says no deal about Jordan. He says he will find you. We left the house with no resolution." Henry's tone was grim.

Blair sagged against the porch rail. She held the phone against her ear, but could form no words.

"Blair, are you there? Listen, we'll figure something out. Walter and I are working on Jordan's defense. You stay well there and don't fret. I'll call again tomorrow, okay?'

Blair sat on the porch until Doro came to the door and told her it was time to come in, that she wanted to lock the door for the night. She came in reluctantly even though she was cold, and told Doro good night. She climbed the stairs to her room, which had been Melanie's room, and still had the décor of an adolescent. A stark poster of Christine Aguilera with the word Beautiful across the top hung on the wall by the bed. Blair could see the influence it had on Melanie's photography: the minimalist black and white outline of a figure with a microphone had reduced the singer to a dramatic icon. On the other wall, Melanie had hung a few of her framed photographs, which in their own way were iconic of the North Georgia she had roamed with her father: Tallulah Falls gorge, a sunset from Brasstown Bald mountain, a gold mine shaft gleaming underground near Dalonega. She had labeled each photograph in a precise cursive script. Blair traced a label with her finger, delicately, touching Melanie's spirit and aching for her company. She took her cell phone out of her pocket and sat with it open for a minute. They had agreed they would not talk on the phone for a week or so because of Dick's surveillance, but Blair could not resist dialing Melanie's number just to hear her voice. When Melanie said "hello?" Blair was silent and quickly ended the call. She sat on the edge of the bed and trembled for a long time.

***

Dick paced the floor, kitchen to living room, back and forth, for a good while after Henry and the other man left. *I'll be damned if I'll let that thieving kid off, just to talk to my own wife.* He stopped to get a diet Coke from the fridge, but there was none. *Where did they all go? Why hasn't someone bought some more?* He drank a glass of water out of the tap, which he was sure would poison him. He went back to the living room, sat on the sofa, and clicked through some TV channels. Nothing was of interest to him, and he threw the remote on the coffee table, causing a slight crack in the glass surface. Panic began to bubble up to his throat. *No, I will not have a panic attack. I will sit still and collect my thoughts and it will pass.* He shut his eyes and sat motionless with his hands folded in his lap. His thoughts calmed and he felt a quiver run up his spine, as if someone's fingers caressed the bones.

The phone rang. Dick jumped up and grabbed it, and sank back into the sofa to take the call.

"Good evening, sir." The voice of Officer Matt Humboldt rang in his ear.

"Matt, hello. What's up?"

"Well, sir, we've got a hit on that tap on Melanie Rutledge's phone, something that you'll want to know about."

"Oh boy, was it Blair calling her?"

"We're not sure, but the call was placed from outside Atlanta, in area code 706. The calling party hung up."

"That's up north in the state."

"Yes, we're able to get a location, in the town of Resaca, home of a Mrs. Dorothy Rutledge."

"Rutledge, Rutledge—I'll bet that's Melanie's mother! What a place to hide. Do you have a phone number for her?"

Officer Humboldt gave him the number, which Dick wrote down

on a pad by the phone. By now, the windows were all dark and a sliver of moon rode high in the sky. Dick glanced at the clock over the fireplace. Ten o'clock. Was it too late to call? Dick couldn't wait even if it was, and he dialed the number. After five rings he was about to hang up when a sleepy voice said "Hello?"

"Mrs. Rutledge?"

"This is she."

"I apologize if it's too late to call now. This is Dick Miller, Georgia Secretary of State, and I've been told that my wife, Blair, may be with you there. If so, may I speak to her?"

"Yes, Mr. Miller, it is too late. We are all retired for the night here. You may call in the morning and I will see if she wishes to speak to you. Good night." She hung up the phone.

Dick held the phone out and stared at it. Did she really indicate Blair was there? Now what should he do? He would not dial her again, but tomorrow his wife would certainly have a visitor. Now he needed a good night's sleep. He went upstairs and grabbed an Ambien out of the medicine cabinet in the bathroom and washed it down with a glass of water out of the tap. He ran his tongue over furry teeth and brushed them with vigor, spitting blood from neglected gums. He looked at his scraggly, graying hair in the mirror and groaned. Tomorrow he would visit his barber. He curled up under the covers of his empty king-sized bed and fell asleep, hoping it would not be empty tomorrow.

***

Sunday, July 29

Doro told Blair over blueberry pancakes and orange juice her husband had called last night. Blair dropped her fork and cried out. "Oh, no, how did he find me?" She jumped up and paced around the dining room. "Damn, I called Melanie last night—he surely had her phone tapped and traced the call here. I've screwed up big time. I have to leave now."

"No. Blair, sit down. You can't run away from this any longer.

You have to face it. And I'm going to help you." Doro's calm voice and steady demeanor made Blair stop and look at her. She slid back into her chair.

"I don't know what to do. I can't go back to that situation. But he's stronger than me, and he has resources—I have nothing."

"No, he's not stronger than you are. In fact, he's a weak man and insecure. He will not harm you ever again. And you have me—and Melanie. And someone else whom I called this morning. And here he is."

A knock on the kitchen door, and then it opened and a large man in a police uniform came in as if he was quite accustomed to entering this house. "Good morning, ladies," he said as he took off his Chief's hat and laid it on the sideboard.

"Good morning, Charles. Thank you for coming. Let me pour you a cup of coffee." Doro touched her napkin to her lips and rose. "Please sit here, beside Blair Miller, about whom I called you last night. Blair, this is Charles Daniels, an old friend of the family, and who is the Chief of Police of Resaca."

Blair had been holding her breath, and had sucked in her gut, but she let it out in a long sigh. "Pleased to meet you, Chief Daniels."

"Please call me Charles. I am Melanie Rutledge's godfather, her father was my best friend through school here. We made a lot of touchdowns for the Blue Devils way back when."

Blair could think of nothing suitable to say, she just smiled and nodded. A lump had formed in her throat and her heart was beating fast.

Doro came back to the table with Charles's coffee. She pushed her plate away and rested her arms on the table with palms down flat. "Now, Blair, we can expect that your husband will show up here today—we don't know how soon that will be. And we don't know what sort of state forces he will have with him or what he will try to do. So we will be prepared." She leaned back in her chair and looked at Charles.

"I have two units of my force stationed nearby to keep watch on the house. I will be in constant contact with them, and they are charged with your protection. We can only hope that your husband will come with polite intent. I advise you to consult your own sense of what is right for you. If you choose to refuse to see him, then we will back you up on that decision." Charles's face was pink and close-shaven under neatly combed red hair. He exuded an air of confidence and authority.

"I…don't know how to thank you…Charles." Blair began to feel a sense of trust and security as the man spoke to her. She almost laughed out loud to realize his face and hair reminded her of her dog, Carry. But she needed to be serious now and decide what she wanted to do. She sat still as Doro escorted Charles to the door, waving to him as he turned to say goodbye.

"Have a good day, Blair. I may see you later depending on what develops. It's really nice to meet you. Melanie speaks highly of you."

Melanie speaks highly of me? That remark hit Blair like a shower of cool water on a parched land. *Melanie speaks highly…of me?* Blair straightened her spine and felt energy move up it, almost in a rush, a brushing of each vertebrae until it reached her head and made her slightly dizzy. *What do I want? I want to be free, I want to think highly of myself. I want a different kind of life. I can't see what that is yet. I have to deal with Dick. He's coming and I will talk to him. I am safe here. We can talk here. He will know that I am safe and that he can't hurt me.*

Blair went upstairs to shower and dress. She looked in the mirror and saw a different face, the same but changed. Her cheeks were firmer, her eyes clearer, and her mouth the shape of a sliver of moon. She would tell Dick she wanted a divorce. She would tell him the story of Jordan and the Porsche, and he would not prosecute the boy. She would move up here in the mountains and find work, honest work. She could open a doll shop, oh that would be wonderful. Her life could begin again. She floated down the stairs on that energy and found Doro in her garden. The dog was by her side, sniffing in the dirt, but he came over to Blair with a wagging tail and a nuzzle of her hand.

They saw a car pull up outside the house and Blair recognized the Porsche. Fear seized her again. "There's Dick, Doro, he's coming to the door." Her voice rose in panic..

"You sit here in the garden and I shall greet him and tell him what

                                    LEILA RYLAND SWAIN

the situation is. Don't forget that Charles and his forces are watching and ready to come to our aid should he misbehave. I don't think he will." Doro went in the back door, shutting it behind her.

Blair sat on a white wrought iron bench with only room for one person. The bright morning lent an atmosphere of cheer, but she clasped her hands until her nails pressed hard into her palms. Her back was straight. She said a prayer. And then Dick walked out the back door and raised a hand in greeting. She did not respond. He was gaunt but clean shaven and his hair had been recently cut. As he bent to sit in a chair near her, dappled sunlight gleamed on the white nape of his neck where the razor had trimmed a straight line. Blair knew that unprotected, tender spot and knew his vulnerability and his need of her, however twisted its expression had become.

Dick did not speak to her for a minute or two. He looked at his hands and squinted up at the sunlight as if looking for some help. "Blair, I guess I need to apologize."

Blair said nothing.

"The stress of this campaign—and yes, I drank too much. I… want you to come back to our home. I am reformed, I promise you. I need you."

Blair considered his words, his promises, the degree of trust she had placed in him that had evaporated. She knew she could never go back to that home again.

"I cannot do that, Dick. Too much has gone down. I want a divorce, and to begin a different kind of life." Blair was surprised how easy it was to say these words, but she trembled as she spoke.

Dick jumped up in alarm. "No, no, I cannot allow that. I cannot…" He made a move toward her, but stopped when she raised her hand.

"Doro told you…what's around us here."

Dick backed away and paced back and forth. "Blair, I know things have not been right for you in many ways, but you know…I love you… and we are a family." He stopped and pulled a leaf off a hanging maple. "And I have to win this election. I mean, how would it look if you left me right in the middle of the campaign? I'd be sunk. You just can't do that to me."

Blair suddenly sensed her advantage. Why had she not seen it before? Of course, his motive was to win, not to treat her any differently than before.

"There's still the matter of my friend's brother whom you are prosecuting for the theft of your Porsche, which is a false charge."

Dick stood still and stared at her. "Why are you talking about that now? It has nothing to do with us."

"It has everything to do with us. I will come back and live in the house with you until after the election. But all charges against Jordan Perry must be dropped."

Dick looked shocked and just stared at her.

"Why, you damn calculating woman! I would never live that down—to let that punk off. No way."

Blair rose. "Our interview is over, Dick. Please let yourself out of the gate to the street." She brushed past him quickly and went back into the house. She watched from the kitchen window as he turned and stumbled down the path. He paused at the gate to look back before he left the garden. Her legs trembled and her back shivered violently as she saw the look in his eye.

CHAPTER THIRTY-TWO

Wednesday, August 1

Viktor was obliged to attend his summer classes at Georgia Tech for another week, although his mind was not on teaching the Russian language and other topics in the curriculum to engineering students. He scuttled back and forth from his apartment to the campus three times a week, gave lectures and assignments, graded papers late into the night like a robot. His mother's news of his brother Alexander's death of natural causes still occupied his mind, particularly because of the implications for the completion of the "assignment" he'd been given by the Russian agent, Oblomov.

He had put the thumb drive that had been sent to him in the election system computer, and that should have taken care of it. The pall hanging over his spirit and laying claim to his sleep sprang from his regret, now, that he had undertaken the assignment. Why did he not resist? Why did he not see that his action would have vast consequences not only in the upcoming election, but in his personal life as well? He was a coward, and now he knew had he not done it, it would not have mattered. But Monday morning quarterbacking was useless, he had acted and his actions had consequences. He could not see what these consequences would be and this disturbed him most of all.

Viktor read the *Journal-Constitution* every day. He searched for news about the election, about Dick Miller's campaign, and for any clue as to what the effect of his action at the election center might be having. He found nothing about that, but polling indicated Miller was in a close race with his Democratic opponent. He flipped through the *Living* section and a small item in a social column caught his eye: *"Where is Blair Miller? We're missing her around town. Rumor has it she may have flown the coop."*

Blair? What had happened here? He had never understood what

she, a beautiful and graceful woman, had seen in Dick Miller, but for her to absent herself during this final election count down was highly unusual. He had no idea where she was and even though he thought perhaps Hallie would have some information about her, he was reluctant to call her. They had not spoken since the day she left him in the Civil Rights Museum.

Today happened to be his birthday, and he expected his mother to call, as she always did on that day. So when the phone rang, he picked it right up and spoke a greeting in her native tongue. "Zdravstvuy, mama!"

"Who the hell is this?" Dick Miller's unmistakable, loud voice rang in Viktor's ear.

Viktor cringed that Miller should have heard his affectionate greeting, in Russian. "This is Viktor, Dick—I was expecting my mother to call."

"Well, I'm sure as hell not your mother. And I don't speak Russian." Viktor heard Dick laughing, a cynical bark. "But I want to talk to you—in English—about this damn election. Can you come over here this afternoon?"

"Where are you?"

"I'm at the office and all my advisors are telling me the campaign is in trouble. I want to hear from you. You did do the thing at the election center?"

"Yes."

"Well, get your hide over here and tell that to my campaign manager, because apparently it did no damn good. Three o'clock. The guard at the door to the office building will have your name." Dick slammed down the phone.

Viktor went over to the Tech campus before heading down to the Capitol. He looked around carefully in the hall where his suite was, but no one was there. He locked his office door behind him and went into the inner room where his file cabinet occupied a corner. In the bottom drawer, under a pile of manila envelopes, lay the envelope in which the thumb drive had arrived through his mail slot. He pulled it out, still looking around to make sure no one had slipped into his

     LEILA RYLAND SWAIN

office. He felt the thumb through the cardboard mailer where he had put it when he came back from the election center. He realized for the first time that he had not bothered to check the drive when it arrived, certain that he knew the contents. Taking the thumb out, he went over to his computer and slipped it into the USB slot. He opened the icon on the screen.

After scanning the list of files on the window, he groaned and slammed his fist on the desk. He closed the window, ejected the thumb safely and tossed it into the desk drawer.

He grabbed his coat and ran down the steps to the front door and hailed a taxi cruising through the campus. "To the Capitol," he told the driver.

***

"Get in here, Daisy!" Dick Miller paced the red carpeted floor of his office over to the window and back, then over to the fireplace and back, waving his arms and groaning. Three men sat at the long conference table, sleeves rolled up, surrounded by stacks of paper and large Dunkin Donuts coffee cups.

Daisy scuttled into the room, arms full of newspapers which she dumped on the table in front of Dick's seat. "Here they are, Mr. Secretary, the evening editions of the *Journal-Constitution, the Brunswick News, the Marietta Daily Journal*, and oh, the *Resaca Ledger*, which is hard to get." She signed and brushed the hair out of her face.

Dick dropped into his chair and shuffled the papers, throwing one on the floor. "Why the hell is the paper from Brunswick here? It's just a rag about fishing and sea breeze." He pulled another one out and spread it on the table. A picture of his wife stared out at him from the *Life & Style* section of the *Resaca Ledger*. "By God, there's Blair in this crummy paper from Resaca. What's she doing up there to get her picture in the paper?" He read from the text: *"Blair Miller is having an extended visit in our town as guest of Doro Rutledge of East Angel Avenue. Welcome, Blair."* Dick crumpled the paper, threw it on the floor, and flopped back in his chair.

A man sitting next to him leaned down and picked up the wad of paper. "Yeah, Dick," he said, "as your campaign manager who's been delivering bad news to you today, I strongly advise you to have your wife return home. News of her absence is getting around, and it's killing you in the polls." He smoothed out the paper and studied it. "The Black community is making a lot of noise about this. What do you have to do to get her back?"

Dick grimaced and scratched his head. He moaned deeply, a sound like a fog horn in a stormy sea, like a hog being slaughtered. "I have to…let that punk who stole my Porsche go free." He slammed his fist on the table, sat back in his chair and closed his eyes.

Dead silence in the room. The manager made a steeple out of his fingers and drew a deep breath, waited a moment to speak. "So you'll let your entire campaign collapse and you lose the election because you're too stubborn to admit defeat in this matter?"

Dick looked at him from under hooded eyes. He did not move. No one in the room moved. Then Dick pushed the papers off the table with one sweep of his arm. "Daisy!" he shouted. "Call Henry—you know, the guy who used to be my butler?" His voice dropped to a whisper. "Tell him I'll sign his damn papers."

***

Doro took Blair out for supper at a local Italian restaurant where she was a regular customer. Sergio, the owner, greeted them with a warm welcome and a glass of wine on the house. Blair sipped the excellent Chianti and relaxed beside a massive hearth where a fire had been lit even though the evening was warm. The wine improved her mood and made her remember a joke from her days at Emory with Melanie. She leaned toward Doro in a conspiratorial manner. "Doro, you know those little baskets that used to hold cheap Chianti in bottles that were rounded on the bottom and couldn't stand on their own?"

Doro smiled and raised her eyebrows. "Of course. That's all we had back then."

"Do you know what a bottle like that is called?"

"No."

"A fiasco."

"Oh, now I remember that. Isn't it interesting how that word has come to mean something disastrous?"

"Yeah." Blair slumped in her chair and twirled her glass. "Sort of like my situation now." She frowned and sighed. "I've run out of options."

Doro stroked her arm gently. "You know, I've been thinking about all this, and I have a suggestion for you to consider." Their meal was served, and over ravioli with Bolognese sauce Doro told Blair what she had in mind.

Blair resisted Doro's idea at first. She had not spoken to her mother since her visit at the house in Atlanta. Deidre had left abruptly the day after she arrived, saying she didn't want to overstay her welcome. Blair had been able to laugh about that and chalked it up to the genteel Southern lady scenario kicking in. The line was one that Blair herself had used to excuse herself from situations that had become unpleasant or which she considered a waste of her time. But she was not sure she was ready to see her mother again.

"Dear Blair, I am so happy to have you here in my house. Of course you are welcome to stay as long as you need to. But something in me tells me that you need to reconnect with your mother."

"Oh, Doro, I can't imagine my mother would be interested in what's happening in my life. Why, she's only interested in her conspiracy theories and the color of her nail polish."

Doro laughed and drained her wine. "Think about it. Now, shall we conclude with the cannoli siciliani, which I think Sergio's wife makes herself?"

Back at the house, Doro went to bed and Blair curled up on the sofa in the TV room. She surfed channels and settled on NCIS because Cote de Pablo, who played Ziva David on the show, was on. Blair was fascinated by her hair and was convinced it had grown a foot since she last saw her. A shaggy mane. She liked it. *What kind of name was "Cote" anyway? The only cote I know is a dove cote.*

Her cell phone rang. She would not answer if it was Dick, but it was

Henry and she put the phone to her ear. "Henry! Hello, how are you?"

"I'm really good, Blair, and I have some great news. Your husband has agreed to drop charges against Jordan."

"Wow. I can't believe it. That's great."

"But…"

She groaned. "Of course there's a but. I said I'd come and stay through the election if he dropped the charges, didn't I?" There was a long pause in which neither spoke. "But I don't want to come back. I don't want him to win the election, and will do nothing to help him."

Henry was silent and the seconds ticked by as Blair struggled with herself. "So if I don't come back, then Jordan will stay in jail?"

"That's about the size of it, Blair."

"I would have to live in the house with him until the election? Is that the deal?" "Yes, and not announce the separation until after the election. But…you can have someone there with you to protect you."

"I swore I would never go back to that house again, Henry." More silence. "Wouldn't a trial clear Jordan's name?" She was sweating and stood up to go out on the back porch to get some air. She felt like she was being torn apart at the seams.

"Well, look, I understand what's scary about this for you. I do. But actually if you have someone there to protect you, just for a month or so, what harm could come to you? A trial would not only be painful—and expensive—for us, the outcome is uncertain, and Jordan would be dragged through the mud. Can you do this for us?" Henry's voice was plaintive, with a controlled fury underneath.

"My mother. I'll see if she will come." Blair's body was flooded with giddy relief. This would work. She could not say no to Henry or let Jordan roast.

"That's great, Blair. And…there are just a few more details." "Oh, lord, what?"

"Well, he wants you to wear makeup, go to the hairdresser, wear pretty dresses, get your nails done. Smile. All that sort of stuff."

"Of course he does."

"So, I'll draw up a legal document for both of you to sign. When can I get it to you?"

 LEILA RYLAND SWAIN

Blair had not thought of her next move. But now she felt clear and certain: she would call her mother and then go to Atlanta tomorrow. She would stay with Melanie for a few days.

She sat on the sofa for a while longer holding the phone, watching Ziva and Tony yearning for each other on the NCIS set. She wondered if she would ever feel desire again or have a sweet man in her life. Putting that thought aside, Blair dialed her mother's number, knowing Deidre was a night owl, knowing she would come to Atlanta, wondering if they could find some way to love each other.

CHAPTER THIRTY-THREE

Viktor had never been to Dick Miller's office at the Capitol before. Their meetings had been at the Cherokee Town Club and at his home and he did not know the campaign staff.

Viktor's skullduggery with the voting machine was purely between him and Dick, or so he thought. He approached this meeting with trepidation. He knew what was on the flash drive in question and wondered what they knew. But he put on a jaunty smile to cover his anxiety as he pushed open the frosted glass door to Dick's office and a woman behind a desk at a computer greeted him. Her brown hair was piled high on her head and she wore glasses with red frames. Viktor always remembered that detail as his first brush with the ensuing madness. She said, "I'm Daisy. Who are you?" Her tone struck Viktor as more exasperated than rude, so he didn't take offense. But somehow his sense of self-importance shrank a tad that she didn't recognize or expect him. *Oh well, my ego can stand that blow,* he murmured to himself as she ushered him to Dick's office.

Apparently a whirlwind had recently blown through the large office with windows overlooking the Capitol plaza. Unruly stacks of paper everywhere, on the floor, on the windowsills, spread out in shifting arrays on the long conference table. Three men sat around the table in rolled up shirt sleeves sifting through the papers as if looking for a lost magic bullet that would galvanize the fading campaign. Dick's feet were propped up on the table and he leaned back in his chair waving a pen as if orchestrating the confusion. When he saw Viktor, he pulled his feet off the table and brought his chair legs down with a thud. He picked up another pen and started beating a drumroll on the table.

"Well, here you are at last, you good-for-nothing pretend Russian. Have you been hiding out in your dascha? Or just burying your head

                                   LEILA RYLAND SWAIN

like an ostrich?" *Bang, bang* on the table. "Come sit over here." Dick tapped a chair next to him with his pen.

The room smelled stale and smoke from an illegal cigarette tainted the weary air. Every eye was on Viktor as he strolled in a calculated nonchalance around the table to sit next to Dick. Dick had a two day old stubble and his odor was rank. As Viktor looked around the table, he realized that Melanie was sitting at the other end. He had not noticed her before. Her eyes flicked over him and looked down at an envelope on the table in front of her. He had not seen her since the visit to the election center at Kennesaw State University, when he thwarted her attempt to photograph him putting the thumb into the computer. Her presence caused a shiver to run up and down his spine. *Why is she here?*

One of the men at the table spoke up. "Welcome, Viktor. I'm Dan Newton, campaign manager, and these other guys"—he swept his arm around to indicate them—"are my hard working staff." He smiled, a tired movement that looked more like a wince. "Things are not looking as well as we want them to now, so near the election. Some things have gone awry…" he looked hard at Viktor "…and one of them is the little job you were in charge of. You remember that, Mr. Durov?"

"Yes, I do. And I carried out that task at the election center."

"Yes, we know that you did. Miss Rutledge here…" he nodded toward Melanie, who shot a wan smile at him "…has the proof."

Melanie pulled a photograph out of the envelope on the table before her and slid it across to Viktor. He regarded it as if it were a snake that had slithered toward him. In a grainy black and white image that had been greatly enlarged, he saw what looked like a half of a slim rectangular object in a slot on a large machine. The nail of a finger rested on the end of the object. His heart beat faster as he examined it. *What's going on here? This could be anything, What do they want from me?* He looked up and everyone was looking at him, waiting for something.

"Well, if you say so, Melanie. I did put a thumb drive in the slot there, and this could be a picture of that, or it could be something from outer space." He shoved it back across the table to her. Suddenly it flashed into his mind: *She wants to tell Hallie I did this.* Sweat trickled down his back under his shirt. He coughed to hide his fear.

"Well, we're not here, Viktor, to accuse you of not carrying out the task. Fact is, however, that there was no effect. Apparently, the programming that should have been on the thumb had been erased. Some strange images were uploaded to the election website that day, but not the kind of malware that we were expecting from you." The campaign manager shuffled some papers in front of him. "We were hoping you could enlighten us as to what happened." His tone was like an icicle, frosty and dangerous.

"I have no idea what happened."

"You didn't inspect the drive when you received it?" "No."

"That seems unusual."

"Look, I didn't want to infect my home or office computer with whatever malware was on the flash. I trusted the source. That's all."

"Actually, the source of the flash has assured us—has assured Secretary Miller—that the flash they provided contained the necessary equipment to do the job we contracted for."

A yawning silence ensued, during which Viktor began to understand the accusation being laid out by this man: he is presumed guilty of having erased the thumb, and of deceit. A noose was being lowered over his head. His mind tried to comprehend the situation and it flailed and twisted. There seemed to be no way out. *What do they want to do to me?* He did not speak.

"Mr. Durov, you can be assured we will be following up on this. You are excused for today. And, by the way, you might be interested to know what was deposited in the election computer instead of the malware."

"Yes, I am interested."

"A series of Russian language comics. Not funny."

Viktor restrained himself and kept his face neutral. "Amazing. No. That's not funny at all."

Dick had been listening intently to this exchange and now stood up and did another drumroll with his pens on the table. "And thus endeth the saga of Viktor Durov, failed campaign operative. We'll collect every penny we paid you for this job, you can bet your life on that." He did another drumroll with his pens.

"I have received nothing from you in payment."

"Get outta here, you fucking bastard."

Viktor stood up and saluted Dick. "Thank you, Dick. Sorry not to be helpful to your campaign. I tried." He walked out of the office, said goodbye to Daisy with the red glasses, and whistled a little tune as he strolled down the steps of the Capitol.

CHAPTER THIRTY-FOUR

Saturday, November 10

Melanie spent the Saturday after the election looking through photographs she took the night before at Walter Dobbs' dinner. She had a contract with *Southern Living* for an article with pictures on the event. Madie and her crew of chefs had produced a sumptuous meal, an array of food and drink beyond any one's dream. Traditional dishes of beef wellington, baked sea bass with lemon butter and capers, savory beef hand pies, baked ham with brown sugar glaze (Deidre thought they'd added pineapple juice and garlic for a new zing), sweet potatoes with a pecan crust, hot yeast rolls and creamery butter, were just the beginning.

The chefs reveled in innovative dishes and outdid themselves by adding new ingredients to standby foods, like mashed potatoes with crispy shallots, sautéed collards with miso butter, and roasted carrots with harissa. Melanie loved the harissa sauce and thought maybe her next career might be chef. *Would Madie take me for training?* She studied the picture of the incredible cheese grits made with Drunken Goat cheese and pumpkin seed. Blair had liked this dish the best. Blair also raided the dessert table again and again for the black bottom pie with walnuts and crème fraiche and North African Zlabia honey fritters. She was not concerned about her weight now that she'd served her sentence during the election, and was free.

Walter and Madie had invited many of their friends as well as Melanie and Blair and their mothers, Doro and Deidre. Tables were set all over the house and especially on the covered patio in the back. There were probably fifty guests, although Melanie had not counted them. Henry and Jordan were there, seated with their parents, at the center table where Walter presided and greeted each guest who came by to shake his hand. Tamila sat with them, and raised her left hand to show Melanie her diamond ring. Was that a look of triumph or a cry for help? *I'm not jealous, really—maybe a little bit.*

Melanie had photographed each table and made many promises of prints to be sent. She held the picture of Hallie's table for a moment, looking at her shining face as she lifted a wine glass in a salute. Melanie still could not believe that Viktor Durov had been invited to the dinner, but there he was, sitting next to Hallie and smiling. Of all the gall.

Melanie harbored a lot of anger about Viktor and his story. She didn't believe a word of it—that he knew nothing about the erasure of the malware on the thumb. But somehow he had wormed his way back into Hallie's affections. Blair had the whole story from Hallie, who had been so helpful to her in her distress. Blair told Melanie she knew the explanations Viktor had presented to Hallie, which made her agree to talk to him.

"What did he say?" Melanie had asked Blair that when she came back to stay with her for a few days at her apartment after the election was over and Deidre went back to Birmingham.

"Viktor claims he was targeted by the Miller campaign to provide malware programming for the election and was told his brother in Russia would be in trouble if he didn't do it. It also turns out he had some heavy debt from somewhere. Some weird Russian approached him at the Botanical Garden and told him this. A UPS mailer arrived at his place with a thumb in it and he says he didn't look at it, assumed it was the thing he had to use. He put it in the slot at the election center at Kennesaw State—you took that photograph. But then there was nothing like the expected malware on the computer afterwards. And Dick was pissed."

"But Viktor DID try to carry out the corrupt task, didn't he? I mean, intent is everything, right?"

"Well, he convinced Hallie that he was under intense emotional pressure, and really didn't want to, almost had a nervous breakdown over it. She took him to the Civil Rights Museum—you know, that funny looking building downtown—and made him go through all the exhibits and experience all the cruelties and oppression her people had endured. He told her it changed him forever."

Melanie was fiddling with her camera, and ducked her head to look at the settings. "I think Hallie is going down a tenuous path with him, but if that's what she wants…"

"She said she really likes him and will see where it goes. The election is over, Dick has won, and so life can get back to normal, whatever that is. But the really weird thing about this story is what they found on the election computer—Russian comics! And Viktor has no idea how they got there." Blair pushed her hair out of her eyes and stood up to stretch.

"Russian comics? You're kidding me."

"I know, it sounds weird, but apparently they're a big thing over there. Hallie told me all the details. This character named Danila the Demonslayer, she has these tattoos that're alive—and they can kill demons. Made from from Satan's blood, the tattoos are, that is."

"My goodness, that's very out there stuff. I wonder what it means. I don't think it's just random. Somebody had an intention to communicate—something. And I'll bet Viktor knows exactly what they mean and who put them on there."

"Yeah, I'm not convinced either. Hallie seems happy with these explanations, though."

"Here's a picture of Walter as he's making the after-dinner talk. I thought it was great."

Melanie turned her camera screen toward Blair so she could see him.

"Oh, I loved it. I mean, for Dick to win the election to governor seemed to me like the worst thing that could happen, but Walter made us look at the issues we have to work on. He acknowledged the massive voter suppression efforts, like closing polling places and purging voter rolls, and laid out the blueprint for working against that in the future."

"He made me feel so much better, to have that election put in a larger context."

"Let's take a walk before dark—it's a really nice day out there." Melanie and Blair put on their jackets and strolled through her neighborhood, arm in arm, kicking the leaves accumulated on the sidewalk, laughing and making them fly.

***

Several days later, Melanie and Blair drove to Birmingham to stay with Deidre in the cottage she made home on a large estate of a cousin. Melanie took the article and portfolio of photographs about the Dobbs' dinner to the editor she worked with at *Southern Living*, a slim older woman with a blunt cut crop of white hair. She loved Melanie's work and introduced her to her assistant, a young man with abundant black hair named Boris Ivanov. He sat down with her to work on the layout of the pictures, writing out captions, and creating space for the text. When they were finished, Melanie asked him about the Russian comic books she saw on his book shelf.

"Oh, yes, I'm a big fan. These are great entertainment, and are quite well done. The Russian culture minister has said they're like chewing gum for people who can't read. But I disagree. Actually, the stories are highly sophisticated, but presented simply."

"I ran across a fellow in Atlanta who had some on a thumb drive that was thought to carry malicious programming and malware."

Boris laughed. "Well, that's interesting. Some are whispering that there's an international spy ring that sends coded messages in these comics and there may be a lot to that. The international skullduggery that my countrymen are up to is vast and complex. But it could also be a giant hoax, a joke they play. I've heard that some would-be spies find out they're the object of these jokes, and it's not a pretty sight. For me, the comics are just something an expat like me can enjoy."

Melanie told Blair about this conversation on the drive back to Atlanta. They laughed and wondered what it was all about, anyway. "Nothing ever happens here," Blair said, "the sleepy South." And they laughed again.

The next day, Blair was packed and ready to drive the Jeep Dick had given to her in the divorce settlement, which Henry had negotiated. "The money Henry got for me is enough to live on for now."

"I respect your decision to go back to Resaca, but I'll miss you." Melanie wept and blew her nose.

"Yeah, I'll miss you—but life in a small town beckons to me. Your mom is taking me in until I can find a place for me and my dog. Maybe I'll find a cabin up in the mountains—I got a lot to figure out. I've spent a lot of years being fairly unconscious about a lot of things."

Melanie hugged Blair for a long moment, and then let her go. She watched until Blair turned a corner and was out of sight, then she lost herself in the darkroom for the rest of the afternoon. She'd taken some photographs at the dinner with her dad's Rolliflex, shots of individual people around the tables and of Walter Dobb's impassioned face as he spoke of freedom, justice, and equality. She thought she could make a statement with these images, a statement of what she believed. Her pictures were her words.